I Was Alive Here Once

GHOST STORIES

I Was Alive Here Once

CALICO

I Was Alive Here Once is thirteenth in the Calico Series.

Two Lines Press
582 Market Street, Suite 700, San Francisco, CA 94104
www.twolinespress.com

ISBN: 978-1-949641-93-6

Cover design by Crisis
Typesetting and interior design by Marie-Noëlle Hébert

Printed in the United States of America

Library of Congress Cataloging-in-Publication Data:

NAMES: Coolidge, Sarah editor
TITLE: I was alive here once / edited by Sarah Coolidge.
DESCRIPTION: San Francisco, CA : Two Lines Press, 2026. | Series: Calico series ; 13 | Summary: "Ghost stories from around the world with a focus on setting and translated into English"-- Provided by publisher.
IDENTIFIERS: LCCN 2025038719 | ISBN 9781949641936 paperback
SUBJECTS: LCGFT: Ghost stories | Short stories
CLASSIFICATION: LCC PN6071.G45 I29 2026 | DDC 808.83/8733--dc23/eng/20250922
LC record available at https://lccn.loc.gov/2025038719

I Was Alive Here Once

Cho Yeeun

Translated from Korean
by Giulia Ratti

Cho Yeeun

A Swamp's Love

습지의 사랑

Translated from Korean
by Giulia Ratti

A Swamp's Love

Water didn't know how she'd died. It had happened too long ago to remember, and at this point she didn't want to know. The important thing was that she was already dead. And that today, too, she was floating on the surface of the creek.

Her days were uneventful and boring. No one came looking for her and no one recognized her. She couldn't even leave the creek, so naturally, she was bored. She passed the time by counting the fallen leaves or greeting ugly fish. That was all she could do.

"Ah, I'm so bored," she complained.

At times she got so bored she wished she could glide down the creek. If only she could turn into a shimmering wave and drift away, from here to there to somewhere else entirely, she could escape this boredom. But nothing like that ever happened. She slackened her body and lifted her head. A flock of birds cut across the sky.

Water knew only one thing about herself: that she'd fallen into the creek and drowned, and so she had become a mul gwishin. A water ghost. A mul gwishin can't leave the creek where it died, a mudang said long ago, having been summoned to cleanse the waters. The mudang didn't know who'd decided it, but things had always been that way. Water remembered clearly how powerless she had felt then.

This meant that roaming the cold, dark stream alone, being trapped with no way out, was the natural order of things. How things were supposed to be. And no one could say why. Water didn't think her situation was unfair. She only found it ridiculous and disheartening. She did nothing and spent her days floating.

Sometimes she couldn't carry on unless she let out her yearning and frustrations. Back then, people still visited the creek. Fishermen, couples looking for privacy, and disobedient children all stopped by on occasion. And Water often gave them trouble.

She would creep closer with only her eyes peeking out, shake her pale arms over the calm surface on foggy days, or grab the ankles of those playing in the water. They panicked and fled in terror every time. At the sight of them running away, jealousy and hatred swept through her. Even though she wanted to chase away these intruders, a part of her longed to grab them by their ankles and scream *Don't go!* Because pranks were fleeting, but loneliness lasted a long time.

Water was jealous of them and so she hated them. After all, only a fine line separated these two feelings. Like the fine line between pulling a prank and taking her frustrations out on people. And so, they kept running away. Then one day, a rumor began to spread that something vicious lived in the creek. People started to avoid it. They said the place was haunted, and no one came around anymore.

The only person who visited every now and then was a fisherman in dingy clothes. Water didn't pull pranks anymore. The vile, dark feelings that had consumed her had dissolved in the current and disappeared.

Now, she had to deal with time dragging even more tediously than before. Her thoughts filled the void between the waves. With more free time, she did more thinking, and when she did more thinking, depression settled in. When she imagined the fish disappearing and the creek drying up, she grew short of breath, as though water weeds were coiling around her neck. At some point, Water decided to stop thinking. She floated on the surface, counting the leaves that fell into the creek and gazing at the drifting clouds.

When a soft breeze blew in, the willow tree on the bank swayed a slow dance. Dry leaves fluttered down from the surrounding forest. They passed through her body and landed on the creek's surface. They were dead leaves, fallen off branches that were still alive. Water drifted lazily alongside these dead things.

*

Then, one of those dull days, Water met Forest. She had been counting the fallen leaves. A hill stood on the other side of the creek, from where leaves and pine needles blew in day after day.

Pine trees grew sparsely between the creek and the hill. The place didn't get much sunlight, and so the pines were stunted, with blackened trunks and sharp needles. There was something dreary about the forest. A wooden walkway cut through the trees, but no one ever used it. Carried by the wind, the forty-ninth leaf landed upon the surface of the creek. Suddenly, Water heard a sound.

Creeeak, creak, creeeak.

The noise had a steady rhythm, like the fisherman's humming. Water stared at the forest. She'd heard this sound before. The planks of the walkway groaned this way due to their loose nails. Back when people still visited the creek, this sound meant someone was hiking along the path. A gust of wind came from afar, and the trees wailed. Carefully, Water approached the bank.

Creeeak, creak, creeeak.

The noise drew near. Peeking over the surface of the creek, Water gazed at the pine trees. She heard the creaking planks and rustling bushes. When the noise grew even closer, Water glimpsed a shadow darting through the crooked trees.

Who could it be? A child from the neighborhood who'd entered the forest without their parents knowing? Or a stranger who'd lost their way? Maybe a cat or wild animal? The noise drew near, then far, and then near once more. The shadow scampered through the dark woods as though on a treasure hunt.

Water kept her eyes trained on the pine trees. But the shadow refused to show itself. Water spun around, following the noise as it flashed in front then behind her. Though she was a ghost, she felt as if something had possessed her. She chased the noise all day long, growing more and more curious about whoever was making these sounds. Before she knew it, the yellow sun was hovering above the hill.

"Time sure flew by today, thanks to you," she muttered, as she stared at the end of the path.

As though exhausted, the shadow had stopped its noisy wandering and begun creaking along the walkway. Any time now, the shadow would appear on the last worn plank.

Water prepared herself for the encounter. Her hair was half-submerged, and she held her scrawny hands up. Whenever she greeted people this way, they passed out in shock, or ran away screaming. The shadow would certainly do the same once it laid eyes on her. No one had ever been happy to see her. Knowing she would never be well received, she had resorted to pestering people. She didn't know what else to do.

Water wondered what the shadow looked like, and how it would react when it saw her. Wait—what do I look like? A long time had passed since she'd last seen herself. She glanced at the surface of the water, but couldn't see her face. Perhaps it was for the better. She would certainly make for a hideous sight.

She lifted her head again. Her gaze instantly met a pair of eyes peeking out from behind a tree.

They were round, pretty eyes. Water grew nervous. But instead of running away, the shadow stayed. Then it moved. Stepping out from behind the trees, a little girl stared back at her with eyes like glass marbles, flashing behind delicate eyelids.

For some reason, Water was scared. It had been so long since someone had looked at her. In fact, this might have been the first time since she'd died and turned into a mul gwishin. Finally, someone was looking at her without fear or anger, without cursing her out. She was defenseless against those eyes. She wished the girl would go away. She raised her white, scrawny arms and shook them, just as she'd done to others in the past.

"Run away, run away!"

But no matter how long Water shook her arms, the girl didn't run. Water was on the verge of tears. Then the girl raised hands as scrawny as Water's and waved back.

"Hi," the girl said.

Not the wail of a beast or the rustling of leaves—but a greeting. The kind one person would say to another. When Water didn't answer, the girl frowned and snapped, "Weren't you saying hello? You waved your hands."

"H-h-hi..." Water replied, flustered.

The girl grinned. Seeing her cracked lips curve into a smile, Water felt a rush of embarrassment and shame. She fled underwater. She sank into the hairlike weeds and hunkered down with the ugly fish. Not long after, she heard the sound of bare feet walking on dirt. The creaking noise also faded away. Only when it had become completely silent did Water poke her head above the surface of the creek. No one was there.

"What a relief," she said, stroking her damp chest.

In the meantime, the sun had set and darkness had arrived. Water lay down between the weeds once more. Even when she closed her eyes, she was annoyed to find the little girl crossing her mind. She wasn't sure if annoyance was the right word for this ticklish, jittery feeling. She replayed their brief encounter. That gaze, that gesture, that smile. They were strange and unsettling. The girl was tiny and her face pale as the bread the fisherman ate. She'd been wearing something that looked like a ratty school uniform.

"Who is she?"

What child roamed a deserted forest? Of course, she wasn't the only one to turn up at the creek. Sometimes people got lost, but they soon went on their way. The same would be true this time too. Water calmed her galloping heart and curled up in a ball. She felt strange. As if she were about to ruin something.

*

The next day, and the day after that, the girl returned. But never at the same time, so Water was always floating when she heard the girl's footsteps and had to hurry to hide.

Sometimes Water hid among the reeds to observe the child in secret. The girl always sat at the end of the path, gazing at the creek with a sullen look on her face. Next to her was a sign that said TRAIL and a huge pine tree, like a jangseung standing guard. She never ventured beyond them.

Covered in dirt, the girl looked sullen even when she mumbled to herself. Did Water look like that when she talked to herself and stared at the sky or forest? Her heart fluttered at the thought of having something in common. That was when a stick came flying at her.

"Ouch!" Water shouted, bringing a hand to her head.

She heard a giggle and looked up to find the girl laughing with a hand over her mouth. Once again, she saw the eyes she'd tried to escape. Perhaps noticing that Water was about to go into hiding again, the girl raised her voice.

"I know you're watching! You better not hide!"

All Water needed to do was plunge her head underwater, but strangely enough, she couldn't budge. Instead of replying, she picked up the stick that had been hurled at her and threw it back. The girl scooped it up and raised it high.

This time, Water caught the stick that flew toward her. The girl grinned as she'd done before. Water's hollow heart swelled at the sight. The girl gestured for Water to throw back the stick, and Water hurled it again. They passed it back and forth as if it were a ball until the sun set. By that time, Water's arm was sore.

"You're always here, right?" the girl asked, panting.

Water nodded.

The girl stood up and dusted off the back of her pants. "I'll be back tomorrow. Don't hide. Say hi, got it?"

Like the day they'd first met, the girl waved her hands, turned around, and vanished into the dark forest. Water glanced at the stick in her hand, then the spot where the girl had disappeared. A faint blush appeared on her pale cheeks. She dove into the creek. Bubbles rose to the surface.

Lying among the weeds with the stick in her hand, Water thought about the girl. Will she come again tomorrow? If she does, how should I greet her? Should I say hi like last time? Water suddenly wondered what she should call her. She couldn't keep calling her "the girl." That would be awkward and weird.

Tossing and turning, she eventually settled on "Forest." After all, she herself was called "Water." She'd never had a real name. There had been no need to call her in the first place. She'd only been named when the rumor of a vicious thing living in the creek had started to spread.

When the mishaps continued, the village summoned a mudang. Dressed in her colorful jeogori, the mudang danced and hurled all sorts of obscenities at her, while the villagers brought their hands together and prayed for Water to disappear. Water prayed, too. She wished more than anyone to vanish from the creek.

Despite the extravagant ceremony, the creek wasn't cleansed and Water stayed where she was. The mudang summoned by the village chief was an imposter, and the two of them split the money they'd collected from the residents. After that, the villagers started to call her "The Thing in the Creek," or more simply, "That Thing," but those names were confusing and vague, so from a certain point they just called her "Water."

"Stay away from that water."

"That water brings bad luck."

That's how the creek came to be abandoned. No one addressed her, so it didn't matter whether they referred to her as "That Vicious Thing," "That," or "It." Plus, she didn't mind being called "Water." It gave off a warm, fuzzy feeling compared to her other names.

The next day, Forest really came back. Water, who had spent the whole day wondering whether she'd return, brought her scrawny hands up to chest level, spread her fingers, and waved just as she'd practiced countless times.

"Hi."

Forest's face lit up with a bright smile, and she waved both her hands.

*

When the sky turned bright, Water poked her head above the surface. The morning was as lonesome as ever. Forest came and went as she pleased, so there was no way of knowing when she would turn up. Every time the bushes rustled, Water opened her eyes wide with anticipation, only to discover a stray cat or a mouse.

The sun started to set. When a shadow emerged from the dark forest, Water took a deep breath. It was the fisherman, not Forest, who came trudging out of the trees with a flashlight in his hand. Back for some night fishing after a long absence, the man expertly set up his tent and equipment. He'd done nothing wrong, but Water was livid.

"It looks like she won't come today."

Water was taking out her disappointment on the innocent reeds, snapping them, when she heard it. Feet walking on the damp ground, then the creaking of wooden planks. She lifted her head. Oblivious to the noise, the fisherman went on with his business.

Forest emerged from the darkness looking disheveled. She raised her head and glanced dejectedly at Water before flopping to the ground without a word. Then she began to kick at the dirt. She looked sulky.

Water was flustered. She had been waiting for Forest all day. Forest had always been the first to speak, so Water didn't know what to do. Forest wasn't acting like her usual self and was clearly in a bad mood. Water wondered if she should just leave, but instead she crept up to the creek bank and carefully tossed a stick. Forest turned at the noise. Their gazes met.

"I'm in a bad mood today," Forest mumbled.

Water pointed toward the fisherman. Forest opened her eyes wide and looked where she pointed. Keeping an eye on Forest, Water moved through the water toward the fisherman.

The fisherman was humming while eating his instant ramyun. Water gathered a bundle of weeds, attached them to the fishing hook, and pulled with all her strength. When the line jerked, the fisherman put down his cup of noodles and grabbed his fishing rod. Water glanced at Forest. The girl watched, her eyes sparkling with curiosity.

The fisherman turned pale as he reeled in his hook. In the dark, the tangle of weeds looked like a clump of black hair. He screamed in terror and hurled down the rod. Water then rose above the surface with the weeds over her head. The fisherman's legs gave out from under him and he landed on his rear end.

Water shook the weeds once more and the fisherman sprung to his feet, sprinting away. He dropped everything—his ramyun, his equipment. Behind her, Forest burst into laughter. It was a clear, bubbling sound.

Water and Forest laughed as they watched the fisherman scamper away. At every stumble, Forest laughed harder, clutching her stomach. As for Water, she laughed because she liked seeing Forest laugh.

"Thanks for making me feel better," Forest said, wiping her eyes. "Can you do it again next time?"

Water nodded shyly. Judging from the look on Forest's face, her sadness was almost gone.

"B-but why were you sad?" Water asked.

"I'm looking for something, but I don't know where it is."

"What are you looking for?"

If it were possible, Water would have helped Forest. The pine forest looked too dark and cold for Forest to wander on her own. Forest raised her head and fixed her gaze on Water. Then she made an inscrutable expression, brought her finger to her lips, and leaned forward.

"It's a secret," she whispered.

They didn't throw sticks that night. Forest looked exhausted, and an odd feeling had come over Water. They chatted about this and that. Strong gusts of wind blew, and their voices were drowned out. When the morning sun rose, Forest stood up.

"I'll be back," she told Water.

"All right. I'll wait for you."

Forest turned around and vanished among the trees.

At some point, Water found herself spending her days waiting for Forest. She missed her when she wasn't there. Even when she didn't hear any footsteps, her ears were constantly trained on the path, and if the bushes rustled, she'd sit up, thinking that Forest was coming. And whenever Forest stood up saying it was time for her to go, Water felt sadness bubble up. She resented being bound to the creek.

"Why does Forest roam around like that?"

Water's curiosity was like a thirst that couldn't be quenched, even though she lived in a creek. She could gulp down water full of weeds, but it had no effect. She realized her thirst vanished only when she was with Forest.

Water waited for a storm. Only when it rained and the creek overflowed could a mul gwishin walk on land. On such a day, all sorts of bad things would happen. Since all lines would be crossed anyway, Water could finally climb over the bank. To reach Forest, she needed rain. So much rain that the creek would burst.

The seasons went by. Water and Forest met every day. They looked at each other, Water crawling as far as the shallows, and Forest approaching as far as she could. Still, a great distance separated them. A spirit's feeble voice couldn't carry on a windy day, no matter how much they shouted. Forest continued to meander through the black pines, sometimes wearing a forlorn look on her face.

*

The rain arrived unexpectedly. For an entire season, droplets lingered in the air like fog, then the rain began to surge down as though a hole had opened in the sky. The creek rocked and swelled. The wail of sirens from the village reached Water's ears.

Water stepped ashore. She walked toward the pine trees, feeling the firmness of the ground underfoot for the first time in a long while. With every step, she left behind a wet trail. She walked on the rough, gritty soil and reached the plank where Forest sat every day. The fragrance of pines permeated the air. She came to a stop between the huge pine and the TRAIL sign. Drenched in rain, the forest looked denser than usual. From there, she looked back to the creek, the way Forest would. On the surface of the water, ripples formed and vanished.

She was about to head deeper into the forest when she spotted a piece of paper. It was stuck to the back of the sign, invisible from the creek. At first, Water thought it was a talisman. Red letters were printed on yellow paper. But when she looked closer, she realized it was a poster. A missing person poster, to be exact. The paper had yellowed with age.

YI YOUNG

BORN: AUGUST 20, 1990

LAST SEEN WEARING A — HIGH SCHOOL UNIFORM WITH A YELLOW NAME TAG

Water gazed at the photograph on the poster. It was Forest. Her complexion had faded, but her eyes that crinkled when she smiled were the same. Water reached for the photograph. A voice spoke from behind.

"Did you come to see me?"

Water whipped around in surprise. Forest stood in front of her. Water was so startled she almost fell over backward. Forest shrugged and smiled, and Water shied away. Her back touched a damp pine.

"I see you left the creek."

Water nodded slowly, keeping her eyes fixed on Forest's muddy white feet. They looked somewhat out of place atop the dark, wet soil. Whereas hers were covered in bluish mold, with green weeds coiling around her ankles like shackles. Forest raised her arms and approached. Water cowered, squeezing her eyes shut.

"How can you be scared when you see me every day?" Forest asked in a playful tone.

Water opened her eyes. Forest was smoothing out the wet poster. She handled it as though it was something precious, despite how worn it looked.

Water felt embarrassed. So embarrassed she couldn't lift her gaze. A fishy smell rose from the soggy soil. She had so many things she had wanted to say to Forest out of the creek, but now the words weren't coming. Was it because she hadn't started a conversation in ages? Unlike her, Forest chatted with ease, as though she were pouring out all the words she had bottled up until now.

"I come here every day to look at this poster. It's stuck all over the forest, like a sign. I live deeper in the woods. Where it's darker and colder. When I left that place, I saw you."

Water was relieved that Forest had found her. She was about to thank her, but then worried it would sound weird and closed her mouth.

"The first time I saw you, I thought you looked very shy. You hid in the creek all day long, with just your face poking out."

It was true. Water didn't know what to say. She just thought it was nice to hear Forest's voice up close.

"Tell me your story," Forest said, cocking her head to one side.

"There's nothing to say. I just live in that creek over there."

"I knew you'd say that."

An awkward silence hung between them.

"Well, do you remember how you died, then?" Forest asked.

Water shook her head.

"You too, huh?" Forest muttered and pointed at her poster. "It's the same for me. That's why I come here every day to look at the poster. I don't want to forget myself. I don't want to forget my name, my face, how old I was when I died—things like that. Not that there's any difference, but these little things have made me feel more real. And then I met you."

At her last remark, Water's shriveled heart skipped a beat. Unaware of Water's inner turmoil, Forest went on, her voice almost a whisper. Water listened carefully.

"Seeing how I can't leave, I must've died in this forest. I was alive here once, and I'm still around. This place might be lonely, damp, and cold, and there might be fewer people who can see me, but I'm still around."

Forest turned to look at Water. Their eyes met for a fleeting moment. Yi Young. Water repeated the name in her head. The two Ys lent a certain smoothness to her name. She thought it fit Forest. On an impulse, she said it out loud.

"Yi Young."

Forest gazed at her. She blinked her big eyes. Water followed Forest's eyes. They darted around, lingering for a moment on the ground before turning back on Water.

"What's your name?"

Water had no memories from before she'd died. But she wanted to say something, too, like Forest had. She was heartbroken, unable to offer what she had received.

She fidgeted a bit and then confessed, "I forget. I can't tell you my name. And not only that—it's been so long since I saw my face that I don't even know what I look like."

"If you don't have a name, we can make you one. You can choose it based on who you are," Forest said.

Water had never heard something like that. Her heart fluttered so much she feared she wasn't allowed to hear such words. She lowered her head. Forest's words embarrassed her somehow, and she wasn't sure how to react.

"Name? A name for me?"

"Yeah."

Forest put her hands on Water's shoulders and beckoned her to meet her eyes. Scared by that intense gaze, Water blurted out, "Okay." And just like that, her fear changed into exhilaration.

"What about Yeoul?" Forest said, after thinking for a while.

"Yeoul?"

"You know, like the rapids. That's what they call the creek you live in. The fisherman we scared last time called it Yeoul."

"Yeoul."

She liked it. Water would've liked whatever name Forest gave her. But more than anything else, this one felt special because it had a Y like Yi Young. Like a matching set. Water shyly replied that she liked it.

"Let's call each other by name next time," Forest said, taking Water's damp hand in hers.

The rain let up. It was time for Water to head back. The downpour had been too brief. Her time spent out of the creek had passed slowly, but those moments with Forest had gone by in a flash. Water would have liked for the rain to keep falling forever. She turned, and Forest, waving her pale, scrawny hands as usual, spoke.

"Next time, I'll come to you."

*

Water often thought about their names. And after each meeting, she promised herself next time she'd talk more, and for longer. She yearned to know what Forest was looking for and hoped she'd confide in her one day. When she imagined that moment, the prospect of continuing her dead life no longer frightened her. It was around then that unfamiliar faces began to appear in the forest.

The strangers looked different from the occasional fishermen, the neighborhood elderly, and the lost children. Dressed in crisply pressed suits and clutching stacks of paper, these men didn't wear vacant or flustered expressions, but rather intense looks on their faces. They didn't look exactly angry, though.

"If we're going to build a golf course, this creek needs to be drained. It's practically useless, full of weeds as it is. I heard there were a number of accidents, as well. We can't leave it like this. It's a safety hazard."

"Factoring in that horrible forest and creek will bump up our costs."

"Let's start by pushing back that hill. We could build a hotel up there. Imagine the view."

It was difficult to understand them. Water was hearing these words for the first time but managed to grasp a few things. They were going to get rid of the forest. The creek and the forest where she and Forest lived—she'd always taken them for granted. She'd never imagined they could one day disappear.

"What are they saying?" she asked Forest.

Forest was still with rage. "Ignore them. It's all crap anyway."

However, Forest's attention was focused on the dark heart of the forest where machines whirred. An orange excavator had arrived earlier that day. Now Forest and Water couldn't talk to each other anymore. The racket buried their voices, no matter how much they shouted. For the entire day, Forest behaved as though she had fallen into a trance. Water grew anxious. Forest might vanish at any time. Water wasn't sure why, but that day Forest looked as though she were fading.

With the droning of the machines, Forest's pines began to fall one by one. The people with intense looks on their faces kept coming and going. Nearly a week had passed since the area between the sign and the crooked pine, where Forest used to sit, had been cleared. The number of pine trees was decreasing rapidly. They were uprooted or cut down, the ground dug up. The forest was disappearing. What would happen to Yi Young then?

Strangely, that season saw no rain. The gray sky seemed perpetually on the brink of a downpour, but the rainclouds always tapered off. Water was afraid. She feared she might never see Yi Young again, that she'd vanish with the trees. Her fear turned to rage. People had been quick to turn their backs on this place, saying it brought bad luck, and now they were causing all this mess? She despised them. It was their fault if Yi Young disappeared. Dark, ominous feelings welled up in her again. Ancient, murky feelings from long ago, when she'd become a ghost. An abyss of darkness swallowed her. In the middle of the creek, which shone a sinister ochre from the eroding hill, Water's dark eyes glinted. At that moment she spotted the man.

"Yes, all's going according to plan. We worked up a sweat cutting these trees down. You won't believe how tough they are. We'll begin construction soon, but the creek will take longer."

He was one of the strangers who had visited the forest. Just like before, he wore a crisply pressed suit with a yellow safety helmet and smoked a cigarette. Smoke clung to him like fog. He ended the call and flicked the cigarette butt into the creek. The banks were littered with them. Water stared at the man as if to pierce a hole in him. Then she moved. Toward the bank.

The air was still, but the creek started to swell. Sensing an eerie presence, the man gazed at the water. A black figure crept closer. At first, he thought it was a tangle of weeds, but no. Long black hair, a pale face, and dark, sunken eyes—the thing moved closer as if swimming.

The man cowered. He wanted to flee but couldn't move. He couldn't breathe. It was like he was underwater. He was stuck in place as though weeds were grabbing onto his legs. His eyes let out a silent scream. A scrawny hand wrapped in weeds shot up from the surface of the creek. Without so much as a final shout, the man disappeared into the water.

Water tightened her grip on the man's ankle. The bone snapped at an awkward angle. He thrashed about as his screams drowned in the current. At that moment, a familiar sound tickled Water's ears amid the splashing. Water covered the man's mouth and rushed to the surface of the creek. There, between the pine tree and the sign, stood Yi Young.

"Yi Young."

Water's voice trembled. She couldn't believe her eyes. She felt as if she, a ghost, had seen a ghost. But it really was Yi Young. Just as she had on their first meeting, Yi Young raised her scrawny hands and shook them.

"I'll be there soon! Wait for me!" she shouted.

Water nodded and waved her hands.

"I'll wait!" she shouted back.

She wasn't sure if Yi Young had heard her, but she was overcome by an indescribable emotion. Her mind was consumed with the desire to make Yi Young smile, even briefly. She wrapped the man's ankles, wrists, and neck with weeds. The more he flailed about, the more the weeds danced, biting into his flesh.

The man bobbed up and down like a frog hopping in a pot of boiling water. From atop a tree stump, Yi Young let out a giggle. Water turned to face her and beamed. The worries and anxiety that had plagued her melted away. The drab world around her brightened, and even the cigarette butts scattered across the desolate banks and forest floor looked beautiful. Water continued waving her hands until Yi Young vanished into the forest. Her gesture wasn't a goodbye. It meant she'd wait for her.

The next day, the man's corpse floated on the creek's surface, but the machines kept hacking away at the hill.

*

Water spent the entire day waiting for Yi Young, her gaze fixed on what had once been the end of the hiking trail. The sign now lay askance on the ground, its pole broken. The planks over which Yi Young had trod, the tree with her poster—they were all gone. She would no longer hear the familiar creaking of Yi Young's footsteps. If Yi Young returned, Water might never know. That was why she decided to keep her eyes wide open. So that she wouldn't miss her. Time stretched on infinitely, even more than before.

One day, a scream rang out from the forest. The sky, leaden with dark clouds, was crisscrossed by flashes of lightning. The whirring stopped at once. The workers, spread out like ants in search of food, rushed toward the source of the scream.

"O-over here! A-a body!" someone shouted. "There's a b-body!"

The workers gathered in one spot and dug up a corpse. It was buried beneath one of the planks. Water watched from afar. White bones jutted out of the mud. Fragments of white and black fabric that resembled Yi Young's clothes stuck to the bones. This was what Yi Young had been searching for. Water quickly scanned her surroundings.

Pushing the murmuring crowd aside, Yi Young appeared. Covered in mud, she knelt to study the skeleton that had once been hers. She stroked the bones and pulled out something shiny and yellow. She lifted her head and looked up. Her gaze found Water's. A bright smile spread across Yi Young's face. Water looked back at her and smiled in return.

The sky, so dark that it was impossible to tell morning from night, let out an eerie roar. Craning her head, Water looked up. Thick raindrops struck her forehead and nose. Soon, ripples formed around her. Then the drops turned into a downpour, as though the end of the world had finally arrived.

The workers scattered. Yi Young's remains were abandoned under a blue tarp. Water opened her mouth.

"Yi Young," she called out.

The rain drowned her voice. The downpour was so intense it blurred everything. Yi Young was nowhere to be seen. But Water wasn't worried. Yi Young had promised she'd come back. Water waited for the creek to flood. Then she waited for Yi Young.

*

A storm, the likes of which Water had never seen, came pouring down. The creek rose quickly. Mounds of soil and hacked-down trees swept from the corner where they were piled into the creek. Water's world swelled. Like a monster, the creek devoured everything in its path.

All of a sudden, everything turned white. First a flash, then a roar. Sounds of a world on the brink of destruction. The creek's surface rocked; the ground quivered. The pungent smell of wet earth pervaded the air. Water stepped on the shore with dry feet and faced the onslaught of soil barreling toward her. The entire hill was coming down. Once high and sturdy, the hill cascaded down the slope like water. The sirens in the village went off. The villagers' cries and regrets reached Water's ears.

"Landslide alert. Residents must take shelter—"

A discharge of static cut off the broadcast. Water blinked slowly. The mound of dirt and rocks tumbled down, and the creek began to fill. What became of a mul gwishin when its creek disappeared? Would she vanish, too? This was the ending she'd always yearned for, but now she was afraid.

She missed Yi Young. She waited for her amid the pouring rain and tumbling rocks. She was certain Yi Young would return. The raindrops stung her face, and she could barely keep her eyelids from closing. With great effort, she opened her eyes. A white hand appeared through the haze. A familiar voice called out her unfamiliar name.

"Yeoul."

It was Yi Young.

"I'm here to see you."

Yi Young moved closer and stretched out her hand. Water clasped it. Two scrawny things tangled together like a mesh of small tree roots. A half-buried body emerged, rising to the surface. Water gazed at the object pinned on its chest. It was a name tag. YI YOUNG. The two words were stamped on the yellow plastic. Yi Young removed the tag and handed it to Water.

"It's yours."

Water looked into Yi Young's eyes, then accepted her offering. Yi Young returned her gaze. Dirt and rain barreled down without end, burying everything—the village, the creek, the pine forest, Water and Forest's worlds, the stretch of land in between. Tree trunks rolled into the creek; the creek flooded the village. Roofs sank, and furniture bolted to walls and floors was swept away. Water watched her world turn upside down. Slowly, she closed her eyes, then opened them. Forest was still there. Water pulled her into a hug. Yi Young hugged her back.

"I missed you, Yi Young."

They called each other's names, and a curtain descended over everything. The racket ceased and there came a peaceful quiet. The creek, the forest, the village were no more. In a world thrown into chaos, Yeoul and Yi Young clung to one another as if nothing existed beyond them. They didn't care what else happened. Covered by the smell of wet earth, they closed their eyes.

Wajdi al-Ahdal

Translated from Arabic
by William Hutchins

Wajdi al-Ahdal

Translated from Arabic
by William Hutchins

The Magic Bin

ZUHRA WAS WIDELY KNOWN AS A SKILLED MIDWIFE WHO excelled in helping women with difficult deliveries. She herself had had sixteen children, nine of whom survived. She remained in excellent health, even as she neared fifty. Short, powerfully built, and strong-willed, she had delivered more than a hundred babies in various villages on the mountain. Villagers discussed her elusive, divine touch. Women in the surrounding villages respected her and avoided quarreling with her, because they knew they would need her help, sooner or later. Even the district governor's wife showered her with presents, since Zuhra had successfully assisted her three deliveries.

One cold, rainy night, a twenty-seven-year-old man knocked on Zuhra's door and begged her to come help his wife give birth. Zuhra had just fallen asleep, lulled by the warmth of her two wool blankets, feeling she was the luckiest woman in the world. When he roused her, she was in the middle of a dream in which she found herself addressing massive throngs of people: women and men of all ages. She pointed at a two-story palace, and a mob rushed to storm that sprawling structure. Then, suddenly, something strange happened: everyone who entered the structure vanished, as if they'd been turned to smoke. The protestors stopped rushing in and retreated a safe distance from the building, frightened. It was Zuhra then who stepped forward. That was weird, even for a dream. She approached the edifice, leading a small group of devoted followers, kicked the door open, and entered. The silence was not just deafening, it made their ears tingle. There was no trace of the thousands of people who had rushed inside only minutes earlier. She searched the corridors and chambers without finding anyone. Then she climbed to the roof terrace, which she found deserted. Since her followers expected her to do something, she issued an order to destroy the entire palace, if only to discover the whereabouts of all the people who had entered it. No sooner had she removed the front door and tossed it aside than she heard footsteps outside. She and her small cohort waited tensely for this person's arrival—ready to mix it up and defend themselves. At this fraught moment, Zuhra woke to the persistent knocking of a young man.

Zuhra apologized; she was under the weather, lethargic, and needed to sleep. The young man, however, brushed aside all her excuses and, on the verge of tears, bent down and kissed her hand entreatingly. Zuhra was moved, and she asked him where his village was. He admitted that it was remote. She tried to back out again, but he besieged her with such plaintive looks that even wild desert beasts would have relented. Zuhra dressed in warm clothes and covered herself with a wool blanket to keep off the rain. Then she set out, breathlessly following the hasty steps of that young man. Her wool blanket was soon soaked and water began to drip from it. The bitter cold penetrated her bones, causing her to shiver. As her breath emerged from her mouth, it turned to vapor. Together they crossed many swollen creeks barefoot, and the frigid water sent a chill up her spine. Finally, the young man stopped in front of a two-story house, opened its door, and invited her in. The door resembled that of the palace she had seen in her dream. She was amazed that they had reached his remote village so swiftly! All the same, she erased every question troubling her mind and focused instead on escaping the pouring rain and warming herself beneath any roof whatsoever. She was immediately greeted by the groans of the woman, whose labor pains had begun. Zuhra cast her wet blanket aside and rolled up her sleeves. The room was illuminated by four lamps that dangled from hooks in each corner. In the center of the chamber, the stove with its live coals provided them a gentle heat. Beside it sat a girl Zuhra guessed was three. Her mouth was so wide that it nearly stretched from one ear to the other. The midwife approached the bed and positioned herself between the woman's legs. This mother was a paragon of beauty, a young woman no older than seventeen. None of her features identified her heritage, but from the extremely soft feel of her skin, Zuhra judged that she was a jinni. Zuhra's fingers sank into this woman's thighs as if they were soft dough. She had heard from her grandmothers that jinn have no bones in their bodies. Zuhra noticed how lofty the ceiling was and how unusual the room's furnishings were. In that moment she felt certain that she had entered the land of the jinn on her own two feet. She felt an instinctive fear roil her blood but gained control of herself and pretended to be calm as she attentively assisted the jinni whose labor had begun two days earlier. Now in her third day of labor, she was totally exhausted, and she and her fetus were near death. The young jinni father got everything Zuhra requested and then busied himself with making prostrations to an idol that looked like an ibex, two-and-a-half cubits tall. He kissed the ibex's hooves, praying fervently that the idol would save his wife and the creature in her womb by butting the angel of death with his horns and sending him reeling back on his heels, filled with remorse. As dawn's first rays appeared, the baby's head emerged. Then Zuhra seized hold of him and gently pulled till he landed in her hands yowling with a sound somewhere between weeping and a blazing fire. She cut his umbilical cord and washed him with warm water. The baby was a boy, and his penis was as long as his foot. His mouth reached upward like a crescent moon, slanting slightly toward the right. His nose, there in the middle of his face, emitted a glow like a star. Zuhra wrapped this newborn in a green diaper and handed him to his father, who was over the moon and began to speak tenderly to him, calling him "Waraqa." Zuhra rubbed relaxant hot mustard oil over the jinni mother's belly and pressed down. After some effort, the placenta emerged, and the jinni mother's suffering was finally over. She stopped moaning, and the flush of life returned to her cheeks. Zuhra collected the remains of the delivery in a clay pot, which she asked the jinni father to bury. Then she replaced the dirty sheet with a fresh one and, with an expert hand, cleaned the remaining blood from the jinni mother and instructed her to nurse Waraqa and quiet his bizarre screams. When the young husband was slow to relinquish the newborn and pass him into his mother's embrace, Zuhra shouted at him to do as she said. The new father obeyed her and walked out. When the jinni mother shyly pulled her breast from an opening in her blouse, it descended all the way to the floor. Then she fed her newborn.

Zuhra's astonishment was visible, and she wondered whether the other breast was as long.

Waraqa suckled on the gold-colored nipple till he was sated and fell asleep. His mother then set him down and asked Zuhra to help her change. From a green armoire as diaphanous as a huge emerald Zuhra plucked an orange blouse embroidered with beautiful designs. Once the she-jinni had removed all her clothing, Zuhra watched her place her long breasts over her shoulders, so that they hung down her back.

Preparing to leave, Zuhra picked up her blanket and was surprised to find it dry. The jinni father gave her a bin filled to the brim with valuable white wheat and told her it was a magic bin. Once she had removed half its contents or slightly more, the next morning she would find it full again. Thus, she would be able to use from it as much as she needed each day, God willing. But, he cautioned her, she should never empty the bin of all its wheat. Once it was completely empty, it would lose its magical powers and not refill itself. She thanked him for this present and opened the door. The couple bade her farewell and wished her a long life.

Once Zuhra stepped outside and shut the door behind her, she found herself standing along a cliff no one could have scaled. Moreover, she could see no trace of a single house or living creature.

The sun had risen, and black clouds had mounted their white donkeys, preparing to depart. Looking around again, she saw that she was close to her village. She told people everywhere she set foot the story of how she was summoned to the land of the jinn to help a jinni whose delivery was proving difficult. She never told them, though, about the bottomless magic bin the jinni father had given her as payment for her services. Every morning, she would take the magic bin out from beneath her bed and find it packed full of wheat. On special occasions, when she was alone, Waraqa would appear and envelop her delightedly before throwing himself on her. Then she would seize him, kiss him, caress his head, rock him, and sing him a lullaby until he fell asleep and vanished from sight.

Anna Kańtoch

Translated from Polish
by Kasia Laganowska

Anna Kańtoch
Krok przed tobą
Translated from Polish
by Kasia Laganowska

One Step Ahead of You

Once upon a time, in a land far, far away, life was simple. Back then, the world consisted of clear, bright hues—the scarlet of royal robes, the white of snow, and the green of pine boughs. Sometimes also other, more subtle shades: the transparent pink of dawn spilling onto the ground or the silver of starry, starry nights. On such nights dried-up old crones would die, tucked up in feather duvets, and golden-haired maidens with complexions of milk and blood would don a pair of iron boots and set off to seek their fortune, shedding tears large as peas. It was not hard to get lost in the woods, wolves gobbled up careless young girls, axed heads fell from shoulders like ripe, low-hanging fruit. In that old world, boundaries were sharp, with edges keen as a sword blade, and tragedy never lingered longer than a summer storm. Everybody knew their place and even evil stepmothers dancing on red-hot coals died quickly, without a fuss.

I'd like to say that one day I found a magical gateway and left that old world like a child walking out the door of their parents' house to fly the nest. But that would be untrue. It wasn't me who left; it was the new, strange world that came to me.

*

If anyone were to ask, Wojciech would most likely reply that he is the most ordinary, boring person under the sun. Monday to Friday he gets up at seven o'clock in the morning, shaves, gets dressed, and eats a crusty roll with white cheese quark for breakfast. Then he leaves the house to catch the 7:35 bus. Twenty minutes or so later he arrives at work, where he spends the next eight hours—no more, no less. His work is boring, too. Wojciech's job involves moving papers from one pile to another. Then back again. He used to know what he was supposed to do with them, but not anymore. Nowadays he just stares at the printed pages feeling like he's trying to decipher Chinese pictograms. The towers on his desk will grow ever higher and increasingly wobbly until they finally—Wojciech is absolutely sure about this—topple over and bury him in a mound of paper.

He awaits this day fearlessly and perhaps even with a tiny bit of hope because, for someone like him, any change would be a change for the better.

At twenty-three minutes past four every day he gets on the same crowded number 109 bus, returns to his empty (and far too big for one person) apartment, and spends the rest of the day there. He passes the time playing solitaire on the computer, crying to sad films on Netflix, and watching out of the corner of his eye as a black mist coagulates like swamp gas behind his back, thicker with each passing day. Sometimes the loneliness, baring its teeth from every corner, forces Wojciech outside. On these occasions he goes to the shop and buys chocolate cookies by the kilo and sweets that give him a tummy ache later on.

This particular evening is no different from all the others except for one small detail. As Wojciech stands by the counter and is about to say the words forming in his mind, he hears a voice to his side say, "Twenty decagrams of Markizy cookies, please. And a packet of gummies."

Surprised, he blinks and turns around. There is a man standing next to him wearing a nondescript gray jacket, the hood pulled low over his eyes. The man grabs his shopping, pays, and leaves before Wojciech gets a chance to see his face.

When the girl behind the counter throws an absent-minded "How can I help you?" in his direction, Wojciech says, "Twenty decagrams of Markizy cookies, please. And a packet of gummies."

When, a few moments later, Wojciech walks out of the shop into the seeping December drizzle, the man is nowhere to be seen. What a strange coincidence, he thinks to himself. It occurs to him that he could tell his work colleagues a funny story about it. He knows, however, that he won't. When you're the most boring person on the planet, no one asks about your day.

*

The new, strange world seeped through into my own reality layer by layer, like mold growing on the wall of a cave until it's impossible to ignore. When a person wakes up one day and sees, in place of a freshly bloomed rose or a key to a mysterious room, an electricity bill on his bedside table, it's obvious that something is very, very wrong. That's why, one day, I headed out from my home, trailing behind me remnants of red, gold, and green. The sky above me was the color of a sable pelt. The mud under my feet...was just the color of normal mud and rusty autumn grass. I walked through a field, chasing away the crows circling me, and I no longer knew who, or even what, I was.

In this fashion I made it to a village, where I was sat down by a stove and handed a cup of warm milk. I found out then that I was no longer in a land far, far away but in Poland, and that it was no longer long, long ago but October 1963. My hostess had golden braids and, deep inside her, a tiny bit of magic—maidens with long, fair hair almost invariably have some—so I fell in love with her, and after a suitable amount of time had passed, I bent down on one knee and asked for her hand.

She lived sadly ever after, and the magic seeped out of her with every child she bore. Soon there were five of them, noisy and mundane as clods of mud. One died in infancy, one ran away to see the world, one fell off an Ursus tractor, one grew up and moved to the neighboring village to live sadly ever after, just like their mother.

The last one, the youngest, I killed with my own hands.

*

The alarm clock rings at seven in the morning, as usual, and Wojciech, as usual, lingers a while in his warm bed, listening to the familiar sounds of the breaking day… The radio plays from the neighbors', doors slam in the stairwell, the yappy bark of some little mongrel going out for its walk rings out, and outside, the 7:04 number 14 tram rings merrily.

However, a moment later something disrupts this reassuring rhythm and makes Wojciech wriggle anxiously in the warm cocoon of his duvet: the sound of quiet steps, the click of the electric kettle switch, and the rush of boiling water.

I must have dreamed that, he thinks, opening his eyes, because there hasn't been anyone else in the apartment for the longest time. He sits up, letting his bare feet fall onto the cold floor, and shudders, also as usual. Everything around him is just as it should be: his clothes neatly folded on the chair, a book from the community library on his bedside table, the alarm set for a ten-minute snooze. Despite this, Wojciech can't shake off an uneasy feeling. It's with him while he shaves, brushes his teeth, and still there when he goes to the kitchen. Next, he would usually take the bread out of the cupboard, smear it with quark, put some coffee in his mug, and turn on the electric kettle.

Today, for the first time in many months, he breaks his daily routine, leaving the open packet of cheese on the table and touching the side of the kettle.

It's warm, just as he expected.

*

I observed my youngest daughter, and as her body shot upward taking on womanly form, I became increasingly convinced that Janina was evil. It didn't make much sense—the youngest, fair-haired daughter was always good—but I'd soon realized that everything in this new, strange world was clearly topsy-turvy.

Janina was trouble ever since she was little. She disobeyed her parents, lied to avoid chores, beat the younger children at school, and tormented the neighborhood cats. Ever since the day she turned twelve, I'd been expecting a bad wolf to come and gobble her up. In the end, since no one turned up, I took the matter into my own hands.

You must believe me when I say that it gave me no pleasure. I did it because I believed it had to be done.

One March day, when the grass had timidly started to pierce the top layer of cold, heavy earth, I took my daughter out into the fields, knocked her over into the mud, and squeezed my fingers around her neck. It was only then, under that rain-filled sky, that I saw how ugly real death is in the real world. Janina died slowly and unwillingly, her eyes staring at me accusingly, the halo of her golden hair lying in a puddle and her heels kicking away at the clods of freshly plowed earth. When she finally perished the world made even less sense than it had before, and I learned the flavor and weight of the word *murder*.

A sea of tears was shed at the funeral: her surviving siblings wept, grandparents and neighbors wept, even the children she'd bullied at school wept. I found out then that the boundary between good and evil isn't as keen as a sword blade, and you don't necessarily have to have a kind heart for people to love you.

My wife did not shed a tear; she watched, dry-eyed, as they covered the coffin containing the body of her youngest daughter with earth, then turned her back and walked away, dragging her despair behind her like a millstone at her neck. I understood then a second important thing: death does not fix anything; it just breaks things. And real tragedy always lingers longer than a summer storm.

I remained in the village for another three years, watching as neighbors, who used to greet me warmly before, now scowled crookedly, avoiding each other's eyes, and previously carefree children kept glancing anxiously over their shoulders. Suspicion poisoned our community; the village was dying, just like my wife who wasted away with each passing day until, once I'd finally decided to leave, she resembled a skeleton swathed in dark, billowing robes.

She stood on the threshold glancing up at me, and in that last moment, when I raised my hand in farewell, I think she must have understood everything. I turned around just once more, at the end of the road, to see my wife suddenly fold in upon herself and shrink, her mourning garments flapping about her in the wind, and a moment later, there she was: flying, thrown up into the air by a sudden gust. I watched as she rose up, her black wings flapping across the sky. There must have been a tiny bit of magic left in her after all, I thought to myself, then left to seek my fortune in another place.

*

By the time Wojciech gets to work, he's convinced himself that he imagined the hot kettle. Maybe he'd switched it on himself, without realizing, before he went to the bathroom? That could absolutely happen. It's certainly a better explanation than a stranger breaking into his home, just to drink a morning cup of tea.

He is mortified when he recalls how he froze, his hand still on the kettle, and timidly threw "Is that you, honey?" into the quiet of the empty apartment. As if he really expected his wife to walk out of their bedroom, steaming mug in hand. Wojciech doesn't believe in ghosts. He absolutely, one hundred percent, believes that, even if ghosts did exist, they certainly wouldn't come to visit him. Deep down in his very soul he is absolutely convinced that he does not even deserve to be haunted.

*

I had neither iron boots nor metal-tipped walking staff, but in certain situations, PKP train tickets were even better. Thanks to them (and their regime-enforced affordability) I was able, throughout the '80s, to travel widely across Poland in search of magic. I found it, finally, in the most unlikely place: among some dilapidated "familok" multi-family communal worker blocks, in a courtyard where the rusty swings swarmed with ragtag children by day and equally ragtag drunks by night. That's where the Mother of God appeared in a vision to Zuzanna P., a fifteen-year-old with protruding teeth. When Zuzanna cried out "Oh!" and fell to her knees, magic slipped into her with the ease of a shucker splitting an oyster shell.

That's exactly how it must have happened.

I saw Zuzanna for the first time on a postcard handed to me by some altar boys standing outside the church. One side had a Bible quotation on it and the other a photo of the teenager dressed in a long white dress, her hair braided halo-like around her head and her teeth orthodontically straightened. Zuzanna was posed in the exact spot of the vision, between the trash cans and the carpet-beating rack: a backyard Madonna with half-closed eyes, surrounded by a weak, but clearly visible, aura.

I paid for the postcard and put it in my pocket, then set off toward the estate that Zuzanna lived in. By then, I was already a different person (or maybe I should simply say I was a person?); I'd donned a human skin, covering it with an elegant suit, the pockets of which contained a wallet and the necessary state-enforced identification documents. Despite all this, I still had a tiny spark of magic left in me, and I think that Zuzanna recognized me as much as I recognized her.

"Good morning," she said simply, when we finally met, her silhouette almost perfectly flat against the red sun, cut out of paper so thin that I could have torn it apart with my hands and walked right through this girl like a gateway.

"I've seen the Mother of God," she added, and I nodded my head.

From that moment on I courted her in every way I knew, from old world and new. I offered her a beautiful, juicy apple (poisoned, of course), a red rose, a brand-new Walkman, and jeans from West Germany. She accepted all these gifts with the indifference of a deity that deigns to stoop down, on a whim, offhandedly acknowledging the offerings made to them. Every night votive candles in colored glass jars were lit where the Mother of God had appeared and the same sort of shine burned in Zuzanna's eyes. Her story of the surprise meeting between the trash cans and the carpet-beater was embellished day after day, taking on new colors until it started resembling a tale from my world. The Mother of God said to love other people, including dogs, but cats especially. And that old Grabowa, the neighbor from upstairs, should get a better old-age pension; Woźniak, on the other hand, should stop drinking and beating up his wife. The Mother of God had also taken Zuzanna by the hand and led her into the future, to a better world, where everybody lives underwater, in buildings made of bright, shining glass, and eats bread and Nutella for breakfast.

People would still nod their heads along to the stories, but for the most part, they had stopped listening. And the local priest didn't want to pay to print any more postcards. The candles by the trash cans started going out, and one warm July evening when their light was so weak that it barely crawled around the courtyard like the fuzzy fur of russet moss, Zuzanna finally agreed to go upstairs with me to my apartment, where the beautifully prepared knives lay.

She stood in the middle of the room in the long white dress; her hair had slipped out from the braid clipped above her forehead and spilled over her sweaty face. She waited, eyes gently closed, and I thought to myself that she must have looked exactly like that when the Mother of God came to tell her about loving cats and Grabowa's pension: calm and accepting of the transformation that this experience would bring. I touched the keenest knife with my fingertip, thought about my daughter's death under a rain-filled sky, and understood that no blade could tear Zuzanna's body apart fast enough for me to get through to the other side.

She whispered my name, turning around her own axis; sunlit motes of dust whirled around her like little angels, but when she opened her eyes I saw no magic in them, just a distant reflection of it, ebbing away with every passing moment.

I put the knife aside and walked out with one backward glance from the threshold. I expected Zuzanna to shrink, her white dress billowing around her, and turn into a bird, mist, or a swarm of butterflies, then the wind to lift her through the open window and propel her into the sky. Nothing of the kind happened; as I turned to leave, she just stood there looking surprised, and I noticed that her straightened teeth had started shifting out of place once more.

Much later, I read about her in a tabloid. The Zuzanna in the photo was heavier than I remembered, had her hair cut short, and in place of a long white dress, wore a tailored suit. She had a husband, three children, and an aggressively expanding network of shops selling toiletries.

In the interview, her mother said that her daughter had always had a good head for business.

*

Wojciech slips through the hallway, safely wrapped in grayness, when suddenly, a surprised voice, silver in color, stops him mid-step.

"Mr. Pietrzak?"

He turns around. The girl at the reception desk is looking at him. Really looking, her gaze like a bright beam of light cutting through the darkness under the bed, where the six-legged, armored creepy-crawly squirms.

Wojciech cowers. Is he late for work? Has he got quark smears on his face? Did he forget to put his pants on? What the heck is the problem here?

"Yes?"

The receptionist—a young, redheaded, and carefree creature from another world—blushes a little.

"I just thought that... It's nothing."

She giggles and Wojciech scuttles away, followed by her laughter. Something just happened there, but he has no idea what. He doesn't think about it, at least he tries not to think about it. He's just an anonymous, gray human being...

It wasn't always like this of course. A lifetime—or ten months—ago, Wojciech had a wife and his wife had a name. Her name was Mariola, that most lovely combination of Maria and Jolanta. A round, pert name that tasted like a juicy, summer-ripe fruit. They were very much in love. The simplicity of this sentence, these few words, always blinded him with truth. They never did any of those mushy things you see on the television sometimes. He didn't bring her flowers; she didn't put on sexy lingerie for him, or prepare romantic, candle-lit dinners.

They just really "got" each other. They went to the movies and out for beers with their friends, hosted barbecues in the garden, supported the same speedway team, and vacationed in Croatia because they both loved the sun... They chatted in bed before falling asleep, and in the morning rush between coffee, sandwich, and bathroom, they exchanged jokey banter. They knew each other inside out: he knew exactly when to offer her a cup of tea after a hard day's work, and when it was best to leave her well alone; she liked to josh about his perfectionism but knew when to stop before really upsetting him. Even their arguments resembled a harmonious dance: set steps, back and forth, so as not to wound, not too much anyway, never taking aim at those most vulnerable spots, never going past that point of no return. Inhale, exhale, chase down the bile rising in your throat, carry on calmly until you reconcile... Wojciech remembered his parents' arguments from his childhood—full of vicious resentment aimed with nuclear precision, scorched-earth tactics leaving only smoldering ruins and sun-bleached bones in their wake. He remembered and marveled at how he and Mariola could quite simply never argue like that.

There was nothing particularly miraculous about it, but at the same time, everything was a miracle.

Together they went through and survived her mother's

illness, the times they could barely afford butter for their bread, and the day they found out that they would most likely never become parents.

They coped. They understood one another.

They loved each other and were very happy. More or less, more often more than less.

Right up to the day when Mariola started dying.

*

I met Szymek in a bar. He was sitting at a table, his long, slender fingers wrapped around a glass of beer, flicking through the newspaper while his legs, equally long and slender, kicked at the bag lying under the table. I asked if I could join him and he nodded, quickly and nervously, his foot hitting the bag again as if it had a mind of its own. I heard a metallic ring in the air that sounded like the echo of once upon a time. But I needed no confirmation that Szymek contained magic; I knew from the moment I stepped into that bar.

"Ghost-hunting gear," he explained, when I asked him what was in the bag. He had the face of a person who'd already fallen onto too many sharp edges but was still willing to challenge life and what it had in store for him.

"When I was little my parents and younger brother died in an accident. My grandma brought me up and she died recently so…I kind of got interested in this stuff." He shrugged his shoulders and finished his beer.

"I don't know why I'm telling you all this," his face seemed to say.

The ghosts at his back said nothing, just nodded vigorously, in unison.

There were four of them: the mother round and warm like a freshly baked roll, the father faking a serious expression with his furrowed brow, the little one—only a few years old—dangling a plush horsey by its leg, the grandmother with the face of a wise woman. I watched them file out and follow Szymek to the bus stop like ducklings trailing their mama. Just before the crosswalk, Szymek subconsciously slowed down, so that the toddler could keep up.

I followed them, closing the procession.

"I want to help you," I said, once we were on a bus heading toward Wesoła Street. Just the two of us, not counting the four ghosts of course; Grandma, Mum, and Dad sat calmly while the toddler clambered over the seats. Children, even dead children, will be children, I thought to myself.

Szymek looked at the window, seeing only the reflection of his own loneliness, the bag at his feet tinkling encouragingly. Ding-a-ling, ding-a-ling… Do you remember the light of the moon cascading down the castle walls? Mermaids lounging about on the rocks waiting for princes and princes-turned-frogs waiting for princesses? Do you remember the dragons, the magic trees, and the mechanical songbirds?

Do you remember...?

Do you remember...?

"Why?" asked Szymek, and I smiled my best wolfish grin. Once upon a time I was very good at seducing young women, and young men are not that different.

*

At break time Wojciech slips out to the bathroom.

"What's going on?" he asks his reflection. In the mirror he sees the same old face that he sees every morning when he shaves: marked by grief, with bags under the eyes and a little bit of stubble missed by the razor. There's no cheese on his chin. His clothing appears to be in perfectly good order. He looks totally ordinary, as usual.

So why were they all looking at him like that? Why has he felt the eyes of his work colleagues on his back all day? Why did the barista jump up nervously when he ordered his usual coffee? And why did Kowalski from the second floor almost trip and fall down the stairs when passing him earlier?

Maybe I was crying again, he thinks to himself. That sometimes happens. It was just the other day when, waiting in line for parsley, he only realized he had tears streaming down his face when he felt all the curious looks he was getting from people around him. But his eyes are dry now. There is nothing unusual about him.

Inhale, exhale. Out of the corner of his eye he can make out a sort of black mist coalescing behind his back, but that's nothing out of the ordinary.

He goes into the stall, uses the toilet, and when he comes out again, he's surprised by the sight of a man washing his hands. Odd, he never heard the sound of the doors opening. Or maybe it's not odd at all; he's been really absentminded of late, forgetting his keys a few times, and even managing to mistake the pile of papers on the lefthand side with the pile of papers on the righthand side on more than one occasion.

Running the water, he doesn't turn to look at the man's face; it's rude to stare at people in a bathroom. He recognizes something quite familiar about the man, though: maybe it's the similar cut of cheap suit, or perhaps it's the aura of sadness surrounding him.

*

Szymek took me along to an abandoned psychiatric hospital, a ruined nunnery, and a castle that was reportedly frequented by a White Lady.

There were no ghosts to be found in any of these places apart from the four that came with us. At the hospital we left the equipment at the foot of a graffitied wall, then lay out a blanket on the rubble-strewn floor and became lovers. Grandma modestly averted her gaze, Mum and Dad nodded approvingly, and little brother watched us with unabashed curiosity.

When Szymek fell asleep, wrapped in moonlight shining through a hole in the roof, I picked up my things and left, this time without a backward glance. I walked away from everything that had happened and that could happen. Me smashing that fragile silver-glass body and walking through it like a gateway. Me and Szymek together in a two-bedroom apartment, shared dinners, visiting his family at the cemetery, watching sports on television, and trips to the mountains.

I don't know what became of Szymek. Did he turn into a bird, mist, or a swarm of butterflies? Perhaps. Or maybe he simply woke up embarrassed, looked for his pants, and got on with his life, donning a suit, getting fat, and forgetting all about ghost-hunting over the course of the next twenty years or so.

In my mind's eye he is still there, encased in moonlight like an insect in amber—the child of quadruple death, waiting to be awakened by true love's kiss.

*

The bus is heaving, as usual. Dusk falls early in December, so Wojciech can clearly see, reflected in the glass, his own face swimming through the darkness along with the other faces, all wintry-gray and tired-looking. He catches the eye of the woman standing next to him and instinctively starts to look away when he suddenly notices that the woman's looking at him. Really looking. Surprised and sort of unsure, she keeps glancing farther along into the depths of the crowded bus, then turning her gaze back to Wojciech, who glances about furtively. The ancient man sitting next to him is also looking, as is that large girl with colorful hair standing by the door... Wojciech suppresses the urge to run off the bus at the next stop and discreetly checks his clothing, his face. No, everything's in order.

So why do they keep staring at him? Their looks stubbornly switch between Wojciech and someone standing a bit farther down in the crush. But there's nothing interesting to see there either. Just some ordinary, gray person in an ordinary, gray jacket. Wojciech has a similar one himself, maybe even the exact same puffy jacket from the Decathlon sale.

Before the bus gets to the stop Wojciech starts pushing through the crowd to the doors. An old lady shouts that he's trod on her foot; one shout is followed by another. The girl with colorful hair blinks, surprised: once, twice. Everything seems to be coming in twos today. Wojciech rushes out of the bus and the cold, rain-saturated air hits him in the face. He looks around, but he can't see the stranger anywhere.

Flustered and out of breath, he feels exposed, almost naked. People keep glancing at him, and now they're quite right to do so, now there's nothing ordinary about this lost man on the verge of panic; their looks drag him out into the light as he resists, bucking madly, yearning to hide again, in the safety of darkness. He'd also like to sit down on the bench under the cover of the bus shelter and weep. Cold, dark sadness overwhelms him suddenly, like a wave; Wojciech chokes on it, but he carries on, homeward, because, as everyone knows, ordinary men in jackets from the Decathlon sale don't cry at bus stops.

*

I had thought that Szymek was the last one, that after him I might never meet anyone else who had magic. I'd even grown to accept the fact. I bought an apartment in the Osiedle Tysiąclecia development, a nice car, and an ugly dog. I went on vacation to exotic countries, and in the evenings, I met up with my pals at the bar.

Then one December day I saw Wojciech on the street.

Him and the thing that walked ahead of him...

*

He turns into the yard and stands in front of the apartment block, his shoes soaked through, rain dripping down his collar and running in freezing rivulets down his back. His apartment is on the ground floor, the windows on the left. And in those windows, lights. Initially he decides that he must have switched them on in the morning and forgotten to turn them off. That's a sensible explanation. And Wojciech manages to believe it for a few more seconds; he grabs onto it like a drowning man holding on to a lifebuoy.

Then the buoy slips out of his fingers as a shadow appears in the window.

Mariola! he thinks. He wants to believe this too, despite everything. Belief in the terrible miracle of love could still save him. Perhaps. But the shadow in the window is a man's shadow, not a woman's. The man from the bus, he concludes, and he's not even surprised.

The man who isn't Wojciech does everything that Wojciech usually does in the evenings: brews tea, turns on the television, wanders around the apartment pointlessly. Wojciech simply stands there and watches, when what he should be doing is shouting, pounding the door with his fists, running to the police station.

Perhaps all these things require too much energy, energy he simply doesn't have. Or maybe he just instinctively feels—knows?—that the other man is perfectly within his rights being in the apartment.

Meanwhile, the man in the window turns on the computer. This doesn't surprise Wojciech either. He himself often stares at Facebook, mindlessly scrolling through the feel-good torrent pouring from the screen.

The man from the bus is not actually looking at Facebook but writing something. Wojciech can see hands dancing over the keyboard and thinks about moving closer to the window, as close as possible, and taking a peek inside. He's curious, and the feeling surprises him somewhat. But the man's already getting up from the chair and leaves the room, returning a moment later with a kitchen stool, which he stands on, spending a few minutes carefully inspecting something on the ceiling. Then he leaves the room again and returns once more—it's like some sort of ritual, everything coming in pairs today—and Wojciech recognizes the object that the other man holds in his hand. He watches for a moment longer, then finally manages to break the spell binding him to the spot, turns around, and runs away...

*

I found him a quarter of an hour later in the local bar, swaying miserably over a glass of beer he hadn't even started drinking yet. I sat down with him, and he looked up at me with the eyes of someone who had missed all the sharp edges in life apart from the keenest one of all. I used up my last scrap of glamour from the olden days, that very last morsel I'd stashed away under my 200-zloty shirt for the darkest of hours. Wojciech told me everything: about how he'd had a wife and how his wife had had a name. About how, together, they received her death sentence, and how everything that was perfect before, so humanly imperfectly perfect, suddenly broke. It started, as is usual, with fear. Everyone was afraid, family and friends. Afraid of everything: of chemo, of a slow death, of what to say when there is nothing clever, or even unclever, left to say. Mariola pushed them away, and they grabbed the opportunity with both hands and ran away, relieved, one after another. But Wojciech couldn't escape, even though he was just as scared. He lost his touch and no longer knew when to offer Mariola tea and when to leave her well alone, when to suggest going to the movies and when to make a joke. It was quite possible of course that it was she who no longer knew what she wanted, apart from that one single thing: she wanted to live, and he couldn't give her that. You don't understand, she kept saying. You can't understand. And she was right; they were like two people shouting at each other from two landmasses that were inexorably drifting apart.

He knew how to share life with her, but he didn't know how to accompany her in dying. Maybe it was she who didn't know how to let him into the dark, cold world that she had been thrust into the moment she'd been sentenced.

She alternated between pushing him away and clinging onto him, between raging and crying. She hated it when he cried with her, and she hated it when he tried not to cry. By the end they both hated each other, and when Mariola finally died in a hospital bed, Wojciech felt relief. Not for long, just a couple of seconds. Maybe minutes. Now he repented every single one of those moments.

He spat out words like offal: blood-red, slippery, and steaming hot. They lay there on the table, squirming and hissing every time a tear large as a pea fell on them.

"And now someone's following me," he concluded. "And I don't understand...I mean..."

But I think he did understand by then. The double exclamation of the woman on the bus, the receptionist's surprise.

"He's not following me, is he? He's one step ahead of me," he whispered.

I nodded.

"And he's in my house now..."

"Yes."

"I have to go back there."

I stopped myself replying. Such decisions must be made alone.

He got up, pushing away the beer, which was quite diluted with tears by now.

"Will you come with me?" he asked.

*

So off we go together: him at the front, me bringing up the rear. And the third one way ahead of us. Wojciech puts his key in the lock, turns it, and goes in. A nervous smile flits in my direction like a lost butterfly.

"There's no one here, I must have imagined it. I've been so busy at work lately..."

The smile is an invitation to share a joke, but I'm not laughing. I can tell Wojciech isn't really laughing either, because his eyes are deadly serious. I follow him in, sit down on the sofa, and he asks if I'd like anything to drink. Tea, I say. I'd prefer wine or fresh blood, but in this world, tea is generally a good choice.

He brings me tea.

I drink it.

He brings me tea.

I drink it too, because it would be rude to refuse. As I sip I think about the magic of numbers. Twos come along more often than you think, three is of course enchanted, and as for four…Wojciech is my fourth chance, likely my last. In this topsy-turvy world it might just work.

He leaves to go to the bathroom, from where he returns a bit later, twice, each one paler than the next.

"I saw him," he whispers in a voice like an echo. "He looks exactly like me."

"Yes," I say.

Wojciech furrows his brow. The black mist is roiling lazily around his feet, but he doesn't seem to notice it.

"I read somewhere once that if you see your own double it means that you're about to die," he states, and this time I do not resist temptation, but repeat:

"Yes."

The unfinished cup of tea cools on the table while Wojciech turns on the computer and opens a new document. He writes what people like him always write: that he's sorry, that he can't go on anymore, that he doesn't want to cause anybody any trouble. He must have realized that all of this is awfully banal because, after a moment, he deletes everything and types out just one word in Times New Roman font size 18.

FAREWELL

And under that, in smaller letters:

This is not the fault of the guy sitting on the sofa.

I think that, as farewells go, it's a pretty good one for someone who, in life, managed to miss all the sharp edges apart from the keenest one of all. So I nod approvingly.

Wojciech fetches a stool from the kitchen, gets up on it, and checks whether the chandelier hook is strong enough.

I could tell him that yes, it will be strong enough. I decide to stay silent. Dying is like a ritual, and everybody has the right to do it in their own way.

He goes into the kitchen and comes back with some thick rope. It looks like rope that, once upon a time in another world, someone might have used to tether a flying boat or restrain a restless genie. I have absolutely no idea how a length of rope like that ended up in an apartment like this, but I have no intention of asking. I know my place. Perhaps ropes are like doppelgangers: they appear when needed, then disappear.

This one does not, however, disappear. Quite the opposite: its thickness and robustness are definitely reassuring; the rope seems much more real than the fragile body that will shortly hang from it. That already hangs from it? The kicked stool falls over, Wojciech thrashes about for a while longer, then dies, admittedly not very quickly, but absolutely without a fuss.

I drink up the cold tea and await the new day, which rises lazily, all golds and pinks, spilling into the room, saturating everything that was gray until now with color, teasing out from the darkness the scarlet of royal robes, the white of snow, and the green of pine boughs.

Only Wojciech's body persists darkly, like an open door leading to the unknown, and I now know that if I so choose—if I'm brave enough—I'll be able to walk through it.

Tomoyuki Hoshino

Translated from Japanese
by Brian Bergstrom

JUPITER

木星 Tomoyuki Hoshino

Translated from Japanese
by Brian Bergstrom

Jupiter

It was just before Golden Week, on a Sunday that turned out to be the day her hay fever cleared up, that Maruko ran into Akane for the first time in ten years. She was at Iris Books in the Taka-no-machi shopping arcade. It was hot, the temperature surpassing 25°C, and the heaviness from the pollen that had seemed packed into her head like so much sand had finally lifted. Thinking she'd take advantage of being able to read without immediately drifting off to sleep for once, she went to the bookstore and was browsing the shelf of 100-yen paperbacks when she heard Akane call out to her.

Akane appeared unchanged since they'd graduated. They'd gone to both high school (Hanabusa High) and university (Okimizu U) together, and Akane's shoulder-length hair had remained unchanged all that time, irrespective of trends or fashion, only the color shifting ever so slightly. And there she was again, her overall style the same as always. What's more, she lacked the small wrinkles at the edges of her lips and eyes that so preoccupied Maruko, and when Maruko opened her mouth to reply to Akane's greeting, all that came out was a dumbfounded, "You're exactly the same...!" Akane replied with a similarly breathless, "*I'm* the same? What about *you?*" Overcome with nostalgia, they decided to go to Bar Toledo, a wine bar in the same arcade as the bookstore, to have a drink and catch up.

Toasting with glasses of house-made sangria, they chatted as if no time had passed since graduation, and in the course of exchanging news about past friends, Akane brought up a particular classmate.

"So, you remember Masuyama, from when we were at Hanabusa 3A?"

"That guy who became a sumo wrestler?"

"Yes! Him! He took a sumo name inspired by this place, Taka-no-tsume, as in 'Hawk's Talon.' He made it pretty far—all the way into the Jūryō division."

"Amazing!"

"He got knocked out of the rankings his first match, though."

"Still! Making it into Jūryō, that's something!"

"True enough... You know, he's retired now, but back when he lost, he went to *Saiō Weekly* and told them that the reason why there were so many Yokozuna-rank champions of *nomadic extraction*—you know, like Ran'ō?—was because of Peninsular influence."

"What? What does that have to do with anything?"

"Exactly, I know. Still, that's what they wrote, they traced different wrestlers' roots back and claimed that most of those *nomadic* wrestlers actually have Peninsular blood..."

"What a load of crap."

"Quite right. I mean, even if it's true and you want to expose how sumo's getting overrun by foreigners, that's not the way to do it..."

"So, Akane, you went to work in Osaka, right? At Zenlock?"

Maruko found herself unsettled by Akane's words and, as was her impulse in such situations, changed the subject. Akane went along, nodding and sighing as she replied. "I ended up getting a job at that security company, yeah. It has locations all over Japan. You work at Kanewan Fisheries, right? I should have stuck to a local company, too. A known quantity."

Akane explained that she'd moved to Osaka for the job, where she was made the head of a new project that had launched just the previous year, but she found that she couldn't stand it and ended up quitting and moving back home. Maruko asked what sort of project it was, and Akane sighed again, explaining, "Long story short, I sold security packages to companies to protect them from complaints from Peninsular types." "That does seem like it could be depressing..." said Maruko, and Akane, relieved, replied, "Right? I knew out of anyone you'd understand, Maruko." Perhaps due to the unease she'd just experienced, Maruko felt relief flood through her; they still understood each other so well, it seemed, despite the ten-year gap in their relationship. Buoyed, Maruko added sympathetically, "Being forced to sell a product by playing on the irrational fears of your clients, that would be hard for anyone. Like your work was based on lies." At first Akane said nothing in response and simply stared expressionlessly at Maruko, then said, "Everyone told me they were jealous, you know. That I was given the chance to lead a project so valuable to society, and that generated so much profit. And they were right. But it was hard being on the front lines, protecting people from ridiculous complaints by people who sit around and do nothing but think of things to bitch about—I tell you, it adds up. I ended up completely exhausted." Akane's expression was dark. *But isn't that what you'd expect, if you're selling a product based on a pack of lies?* Maruko thought, but she stopped herself from putting the thought into words. She could just imagine the response: *That's just what those Peninsular types do! They brainwash sympathizers like you, working behind the scenes while you do their dirty work—I can see they've already done a number on you, Maruko, if you're thinking like this...* She decided to change the subject again instead.

"Are you still with Nishino?" asked Maruko, referring to the guy Akane had dated when they'd been classmates. Akane replied peevishly, "When do you think this is? We broke up a long time ago. We were just students playing house anyway." She continued muttering to herself: now that she was an adult, she was looking for someone who was husband material, but every guy failed to measure up—it felt like there was no one out there for her.

Truth be told, Maruko had had the same reservations about Yugure, the guy she was currently seeing, and she was sick of it too. "It feels like there's not much we can do about it, though. It bothers me when people pester me about getting married—it shouldn't be that big a deal if I never do!" Akane nodded, saying, "Yeah, I can see that," then added, "But thinking about getting old alone, it makes me sad." "Why don't we become roommates, then? I think that's going to be a more and more common way to deal with old age anyway." Maruko was only half-joking. Akane laughed, replying, "That sounds fun!" Then she grew serious. "But there's *productivity* to consider."

"Productivity?"

"Well, the two of us can't make a baby ourselves!"

"You want children, Akane?"

"Not really, it's more that I'd feel guilty about lowering the Japanese population."

It was Maruko's turn to laugh. "Wha-at? Don't exaggerate!"

Akane's reply was indignant. "I'm not the one exaggerating..."

Things had reached the point of discomfort again.

Unable to hold back any longer, Maruko said, "You've changed, Akane." The words came out on their own, like a reflex.

"*I've* changed? If anything, *you're* the one who's changed, Maruko."

"I haven't changed."

"You have. I say things and the way you respond...there's something off. Things you would have responded to before, now, well—it's like you're not there for me at all."

Maruko felt sick. She decided to be as clear as possible. "How can I be there for you when you say things that the Akane I knew would never have said?"

Akane replied angrily. "*That's* what's changed! That right there! You've become rigid, Maruko. You used to be more flexible. You'd read the room and respond accordingly, smooth things over. I always admired that about you. Now you're bullheaded. Unbending. It freaks me out."

"Akane, do you remember what we said to each other when we graduated? We said we didn't want to just go along with things, even after school. We wanted to stay true to ourselves. I always imagined us living that way, unswayed by what others might think or say. I thought that was what made us such good friends, that we were two people who did our own thing, who went our own way. Sure, becoming an adult meant I had to compromise on some things, we all have to do that. But I do it so I don't have to compromise *everything*. I'm the same person at heart. I haven't lost myself by going along with things. But it seems you have, Akane. You've lost yourself and gone somewhere I can't follow."

"You know who you sound like? Those *complaining types* I had to deal with!"

Maruko looked at Akane's face, so familiar in every way, and felt she was talking to a complete stranger. Who was this person spouting buzzwords and parroting whatever "common sense" was in the air—surely this was everything the Akane she knew before would have despised. Where had she gone? The girl who always did her own thing, who never went along with anything she didn't truly believe? Maruko was gripped by the sudden desire to find out what had happened to her old friend, at any cost, even if it meant throwing their whole relationship away. Not only for herself: it felt like a problem Akane needed to face directly.

However, as they sat staring at each other, Maruko looked into Akane's glassy, expressionless eyes and realized that any such effort would be in vain. They no longer spoke the same language. Powerlessness washed over her, a wave of exhaustion that drained the strength from her body, starting at her back and continuing down through her legs. Maruko suggested they go, and Akane nodded. They split the bill and left.

Akane and Maruko walked home together down the road that ran along the train tracks. Akane chattered cheerfully about the new breathing exercises she'd been learning in her free time, how calming they were, how good they made her feel, going on and on as if the earlier awkwardness had never happened. "Whenever I feel on the verge of giving in to anger or hopelessness, I do the exercises and feel immediately better, calm and tranquil, like I've had a little epiphany," Akane explained, and then she gave a demonstration, urging Maruko to give it a try too. Maruko did as she was told, but just as she was breathing in and out, the warning bell of the railroad crossing beside them began to clang. Akane responded suddenly, hurrying across the tracks without another word.

Maruko felt completely abandoned. True, Akane's place was just across the tracks, and Maruko's a bit farther down, so this was the natural place to part ways. But it felt more like Akane had suddenly leapt onto a train and disappeared with it.

And indeed, the real train soon arrived, buffeting Maruko with the wind of its passage, and once the warning bell's clanging stopped and the yellow-and-black-striped bar lifted, Akane was nowhere to be seen.

Maruko got home, and finding herself still a bit rattled, she decided to call up Fumiyo, another friend from high school with whom she grabbed a bite to eat every few months, and tell her about the Akane Incident. Fumiyo responded with an unnaturally long silence, and then finally said, "I don't think Akane's changed much at all, actually." Maruko felt herself start to dissociate at Fumiyo's words. Afraid she was about to fall to pieces completely, Maruko hurriedly began to make excuses for her remark. "Well, it's like, sometimes *not* changing can feel like a change, you know? I guess I imagined that Akane had changed over the years, but it turns out she *didn't*, so that's what threw me off..." They made plans to have lunch together at the end of the month, and Maruko hung up the phone.

Maruko turned off all the lights in the apartment and walked over to the southwest-facing window, sticking her head out to look at the night sky. An ivory point of light shone brightly in front of her. It wasn't twinkling, which she'd heard meant it was a planet, not a star. Could it be Jupiter? Low and to the west, the thin crescent moon appeared like a rip in the sky. She heard the distant clanging of the train crossing. Still feeling abandoned, she thought about calling Yugure, but then remembered he was at kendō practice and would surely go out drinking with his teammates afterward. A call from her would only irritate him.

The next day at work, Maruko was eating her homemade lunch in Kaki-no-ike Park with her coworker Kiyohara when she decided to bring up the Akane Incident and Fumiyo's response. It seemed like a safe choice—they chatted over lunch together every day, so surely Kiyohara would understand. But as Maruko began her story, she noticed Kiyohara was no longer making eye contact, studying the ground instead. Soon it was too painful to keep talking—Kiyohara remained silent, and Maruko too fell quiet. "You agree with Akane, don't you?" she murmured.

"I've always been your friend, Maruko," said Kiyohara, her gaze still fixed on the ground. Maruko realized, suddenly, that she was an outsider at the office, that her coworkers talked about her behind her back. She'd sensed as much before, but she'd consciously decided not to think about it. To have Kiyohara, whom she'd always assumed to be on her side, respond this way threw the truth into undeniable relief.

"You think I've changed?" asked Maruko. Kiyohara kept silent for a little while longer, and then raised her head to look Maruko in the eye. "You really don't see it? You've changed so much, become so strange. You've left us all behind. Even just having lunch with you feels dangerous." Anger colored Kiyohara's voice and gaze. *Are you so self-centered that you don't even notice how much I've endured by remaining at your side? The others may very well think I'm like you! Have you no sense of shame or responsibility for the risks I've taken?* These were the thoughts seemingly simmering just beneath her words.

Maruko felt as though she'd lost her footing, as if she'd just been thrown from a watchtower. She and Kiyohara had always vented to each other about colleagues and bosses who pretended to hold strong, consistent views while twisting and turning to match whichever way the wind was blowing at the company. Maruko had always assumed that a contempt for hypocrisy was what bonded them—their shared opinion that this lack of integrity would actually cost the company in the long run, that it was always better to stay true to yourself on the job because to do otherwise was tantamount to selling your soul. So clearly it was Kiyohara, not Maruko, who'd changed. She'd succumbed to the pressure; she'd sold her soul. Those who sell their souls look at those who haven't and say, "Oh, they've changed!" As if, having boarded a train, they were to accuse those left on the platform of moving.

It was useless to ask someone who sold their soul to go back to the way they were; there's no longer any there there to return to. "I'm sorry for the trouble I've caused you," said Maruko, before packing up her lunchbox and returning to the office alone. Happily, she had meetings that took her out of the office all afternoon, so she was able to finish work without running into Kiyohara again.

Unable to stand being alone at her place any longer, Maruko decided to email Yugure and arrange dinner with him at his apartment. That night, she tried not to discuss the recent chain of events with Yugure, afraid of only more repeated awkwardness. But then it occurred to her that, whether or not he was really husband material, there was no point being in a relationship if she couldn't even tell him about the things that were bothering her. And so she screwed up her courage and brought up her recent troubles. As it turned out, though, even these faint hopes ended up dashed. "We've never really talked like this, have we?" said Yugure. "I'd always figured we were both adult enough to know that if we talked about this kind of thing one of us would end up getting hurt and we might break up, and so we just avoided it. Or at least, that was how I understood things. Guess not. Which makes me wonder why I went to the trouble of being so careful in the first place." His eyes were like those of a doll. Maruko felt like she was the only one with eyes made of flesh, eyes that would rot in her head and ooze from their sockets once she died. She felt polluted, disgusting. "So why are we together at all, then?" she asked. Yugure laughed bleakly, as if appalled by her question. "Because I'm all you have, Maruko! When we first got together, we had an unspoken understanding that we were both just killing time till we met other people, right? But then you started changing. You started changing so quickly it seemed impossible you could ever find anyone else. Sometimes I feel like I'm dating someone who speaks an entirely different language from me, who's from a different civilization, a different race. I've been living in fear that one day you'd broach the subject of marriage—what on earth would I do then? Our children would be like *half-breeds*! I know I sound cruel, but what if we thought of it a different way? Like I was returning you to your brethren in that other civilization, that other world? Wouldn't I be saving you then? I haven't been able to decide on the right thing to do. But now seems like a good opportunity to finally lay all the cards on the table. And you know, no matter how much you change or how strange you become, Maruko, I'll still like you." Yugure reached out to take Maruko's hand as he finished speaking. Maruko was chilled by Yugure's shapeshifting formlessness; the impenetrability of his thinking exhausted her, as if she'd been carefully guessing at the innermost thoughts of a slug. She decided to return to her place rather than spend the night there. As she waited for sleep to arrive, she heard the distant clanging of the railroad crossing. It made her think of Jupiter.

Early the next morning, Maruko decided to ride her bike over to Akane's house before work. Partially because she didn't know her phone number or email address, but also because she couldn't shake the feeling that if only they could meet face to face one more time they might repair their friendship. And if that happened, perhaps there was hope of repairing all the other relationships in her life that seemed to be falling apart. Maybe a life out of joint was like a misbuttoned shirt—the only way to fix it was to go back and undo the original mistake.

The woman who answered the door was Akane's mother, whom Maruko remembered meeting countless times back when she was a student. "Is Akane home?" asked Maruko, and Akane's mother's expression darkened, her eyes turning hollow and empty. "Akane passed away last year," she said. Now it was Maruko's face that fell as she muttered, half to herself, "But I just ran into her on Sunday—we had a drink together and talked until evening. We even split the bill!" Akane's mother answered, "Is that so? Well, you're not the only one. Other old friends of hers have come here like you, saying they ran into her on the street and wanting to pay a visit. I can't have you in to offer incense, though—we don't have a shrine for her." "Was she sick? Was it an accident?" Akane's mother snorted softly as if amused by the question, though her overall expression remained unchanged. "She walked onto the train tracks." Maruko didn't need to ask more. She already knew what had led up to Akane's death, as if she'd witnessed it with her own eyes. The day before yesterday, Akane herself had shown her.

Perhaps it was just that, after undergoing such a radical transition, Akane had envied Maruko and wanted her to change too. Or perhaps she'd simply wanted to communicate to Maruko that she'd never wanted to change at all. The despair that filled her heart lingered even after she died, and she needed Maruko to take some of it on for her, even just a little. And she succeeded—a handful of Akane's sorrow was now Maruko's. But even this tiny amount was too much, enough to alter Maruko's entire destiny. She had the feeling that if she wandered the streets again, sooner or later she'd run into Akane once more.

Maruko returned home and began putting her sluggish body through the motions of getting ready for work. Before she did, though, she sprinkled herself with purifying salt, then instantly despised herself for the impulse. Arriving seven minutes late to work, she found that the morning assembly was already half over. Even so, no one deigned to look at her. She wished for a roomful of sharp, reproachful gazes—at least then things would be clear.

Kiyohara was nowhere to be found. Maruko's heart hurt at the thought that it might be her fault. She threw herself into her work all morning in an attempt to ward off the ominous presentiment growing within her, but it didn't work, and the feeling just became more and more intense as she ate lunch alone in

Kaki-no-ike Park. Unable to stand it anymore, she went back to the office, and turning to Kimura at the desk beside hers, asked, "Did Kiyohara take the day off?" Kimura seemed truly dumbfounded by the question, staring at her until he finally found the words to say, "Are you okay, Kamata-san?" Without waiting for an answer, he continued. "Kiyohara passed away three years ago. They all did, together—Kiyohara and Nagi and Mrs. Yuki and Nogi and Yūsuke and Little Takagami, along with their commanding officer. You don't remember?" Maruko was at a complete loss. They'd just had lunch together yesterday! Like they did every weekday, except Thursdays! They'd gone out for drinks Friday night at Uomasa! They'd taken a trip together last March to Ishigaki-jima! Flooded with vivid memories of their time together, Maruko couldn't bring herself to reply to Kimura's question, so he went on. "You know, I get it. I used to see her all the time, too, at work. I even talked to her at the cafe, just like normal. And not just me—Kiyama was there, too, the three of us talking. That was about six months after she drowned. It's been three years now, so I thought she'd made it to the other side by now. But maybe not. Or maybe she just returned for a little visit. Though the Bon festival is still a ways away." Kimura turned back to his work.

Maruko went back to her work as well, performing her duties while experiencing such a complete break with reality that it was as if she were made of vapor, not flesh. She had some overtime tasks to complete, so it wasn't until after ten that she headed to Yugure's place. She'd emailed to tell him she was coming over but received no answer. Figuring that the ill feelings of the previous evening had yet to be smoothed over, Maruko decided that it would be best to go over right then and address things head on, even as she felt her heart sinking along with the setting sun. She used the key he'd given her to enter the dark apartment only to find he wasn't there. It was unusual for Yugure's city hall job to keep him late, so she figured he must have gone out for a drink. Perhaps he couldn't bring himself deal with their hopeless relationship sober. Maruko searched high and low throughout the apartment, but he didn't seem to have left a note or anything else for her.

She took a shower, borrowed a pair of his pajamas, heated up some cold pizza and washed it down with a beer, then turned off all the lights and went to the window to check if Jupiter and the crescent moon still hung where she'd left them the night before. She borrowed Yugure's computer to do a little shopping, ordering some compression stockings that were on sale. Soon it was one in the morning, then two—obviously something was wrong. Figuring that an email wouldn't do, Maruko tried calling him.

The call went through. But the voice on the other end belonged to another man, not Yugure. Maruko found herself unable to speak. “Hello? Hello?” repeated the voice, and then it said, “Maruko, is that you?” Faced with her continued silence, the voice went on. “This is Gyōten, Yugure’s brother.” Maruko finally found her words. “His brother?”

“It’s been a while, hasn’t it? How are you?”

“I’m all right. Well, I guess not *that* all right...”

“You wouldn’t be calling like this if you were all right, I suppose.”

“That’s one way of putting it. Is Yugure with you? Is there some reason why he can’t come to the phone himself?”

Now it was Gyōten’s turn to be silent. “Maruko...” he said, finally, as if on the verge of disclosing some important news. Maruko, guessing what that might be, interrupted him. “Yugure’s dead, isn’t he?”

“If you knew already, why did you call?”

“Why is everyone around me dying all of sudden?” replied Maruko, though she knew she was asking the wrong person.

“Maruko, I understand you’re in shock, but you’ve got to accept reality. It’s been six months since Yugure died in the Battle of the Sea of Japan. Don’t you remember when his body came home? You spent the night with him in the shelter, holding his hand, talking to him. You said it felt like he could still hear you.”

"Battle of the Sea of Japan? What are you talking about?"

"I've told you a thousand times, but I guess your memory keeps resetting to zero. The Peninsula and the Mainland became so tyrannical and threatening, something had to be done, and so we Islanders were forced to unite against them!"

"What conflict? Where? All I do is go to work every morning and then come home and eat dinner with Yugure! Just a normal, boring life!"

"That's how it was for a while, it's true. But those days are long gone. You're stuck there, Maruko. Living in the past. The time has come for you to open your eyes and face the outside world."

"That's what I'm trying to do! How much farther 'outside' do I have to go? Outer space?"

"Ask yourself this, Maruko—why do you suppose you're so alone?"

"I wasn't, till yesterday! I'm just trying to figure out what's going on!"

"They were all drafted, Maruko! Don't you remember? Everyone your age ended up going to war, men and women alike. They sacrificed themselves to protect Island Honor! And then they melted into air and became Guardian Spirits. Yugure included. There was a time when our cities were filled with just old people and children—strangely peaceful, really.

At least till the drones came. You were pregnant when all this happened, that's why you escaped the draft."

"I don't have a child."

"You lost it. The doctor said it was the stress of Yugure going to war, but I know the truth. I know what you did. You didn't want your baby to grow up to be a soldier, so you stole its future with your own hands. Of course you feel guilty. Of course you can't face reality. You deny what you did by denying everything, by living in the past, as if none of it ever happened at all. To absolve yourself."

However horrible reality became, was it really possible to live in such total denial? It certainly didn't seem like a problem of perception to her—she'd simply been living her life up till yesterday surrounded by people she was only now being told were all dead.

"I'm standing in Yugure's apartment right now. I can see the quiet streets outside through the window. I can see the moon and the constellations and Jupiter like always. No sign of war anywhere."

"Is that so? Maybe you should turn around and take a look behind you."

The voice seemed to be coming from outside the phone. Maruko turned to look behind her. Gyōten was there, dressed in pajamas. He was standing in a foyer with a vaulted ceiling that went all the way up to the second floor. She could see light filtering through a stained-glass window behind him. It had the fierce figure of Niō, the Buddhist guardian spirit, outlined within it. She recognized the room as the foyer of Yugure's parents' house from the one time she'd accompanied him there on a visit.

"Do you get it now? How what you think is your everyday life is just a manifestation of what you want to see?"

Gyōten sat down where he was, cross-legged.

"So where am I, really? These kinds of things don't happen in reality. If everyone around me's dead, wouldn't that mean I'm dead, too? But I'm not!"

Maruko felt her existence start to evaporate as she spoke, as if her very self was melting into the air around her.

"How far are you going to take this know-nothing act? Who do you think is still around? You think you're alive? Your parents, your brother, my mother, my wife, my daughter, even me—we're all dead! You don't remember how it was? The hell we found ourselves in? The Battle of the Sea of Japan ended in defeat. They broke through the frontlines and filled our skies with bomb-dropping drones, so many it was as if storm clouds were blotting out the sun. The days were black as night, and the air was filled with the sound of them, a loud, low hum like a million priests chanting sutras all at once. We tried to load the children and old people onto boats to save them, but just as we were sending them off, another attack came from above. No one was spared. I'm sure you died in an instant, Maruko. No warning, no time to prepare. Not even time to notice you were dead. Or accept it."

By the end of his monologue, Gyōten's voice had grown soft, his head bowed as if he were speaking more to himself than Maruko, and then he stopped speaking entirely and looked back up at her. It was as if someone had taken Yugure's face and remolded it with their hands, making his eyebrows more prominent, his lips thicker, his nose a little flatter... Without quite realizing what she was doing, Maruko brought her hand up to touch her face, then reached out to touch Gyōten's arm. It was flesh; they were both still flesh.

"The Islands were nearly wiped out. The Mainland suffered enormous losses, too, but there were so many more of them to begin with. Our islands fell one after the other, and they became like islands in a dream. Everything on them—the buildings, the trees, every living thing—was preserved as ruins. The air was filled with poison and the smell of rot, enough to suffocate any remaining life. Every animal or bird that could escape did. Yet, even though everything's in ruins, it's still there—the way the world looked around us in our everyday lives is much the same. And so there are more and more people like you, Maruko.

People who can't accept that they've died, who go about living as if nothing happened. There are so many that it can really feel like life is still going on."

"Is Yugure one of them too?"

"He may very well be."

"And so he's a Guardian for real, then. That's what you said, right? That those who sacrificed themselves in battle melted into air and became Guardian Spirits. But now you're saying that it's just that they can't accept their own deaths? If the Islands are destroyed, what's left for them to protect?"

"Maybe just other dead people. Maybe that's it. I don't know, really."

"So the dead end up watching over the dead? Were you sent off to war too? You're only two years older than Yugure, if he was drafted you would have been drafted as well."

"I was. I died in battle too."

"So that means you're a Guardian Spirit, too, right? And yet here you are, lecturing me like this. You're just the same as me, wandering the face of the earth unable to accept your own death! And why is that, do you suppose? Why can't we accept our deaths? Because they're unacceptable, that's why! We all got on the same train together, after all. Packed in the same train, rocking and swaying together as we all headed the same direction. Who would think that the train was headed toward total destruction? Who would think we'd end up destroyed along with it, all of us together like that? Am I right? What do you think? Say something!"

But Gyōten's face had lost all expression, as if his soul had left his body. Finally, he muttered, "That's true, I suppose. But why did it happen like that...?" Then he rose to his feet, turned his back on Maruko, slipped on his sandals, and walked out the door. They were no longer beneath the vaulted ceiling of the foyer, she realized. She walked to the window and stuck her head out. After a moment, she caught sight of Gyōten walking away from her, still in his pajamas, his steps listless and slow; he was illuminated by the blue-white light of an LED streetlamp. At one point he stopped and lit a cigarette. Then he started walking again. She saw the ivory glow of Jupiter hanging in the sky above him, exactly where she'd last seen it, unblinking, untwinkling, eternal.

She heard the key turn in the door beside her. Gyōten had left without locking the door, but it seemed to be locked again. The knob turned, and someone tried to pull it open from the outside but to no avail; the door was still locked. She heard a voice mutter. *What the hell?* The key turned in the lock again. This time, the door swung open. He stepped into the light of the apartment. It was Yugure.

Salomat Vafo

Translated from Uzbek
by Sabrina Jaszi

Salomat Vafo

Sochi yoyiq xotinlar

THE LOOSE HAIRED WOMEN

Translated from Uzbek
by Sabrina Jaszi

The Loose-Haired Women

UNDETERRED BY HER BROTHERS WHO TOLD HER TO "SIT, STAY the night, sister," Zarina thought of her nursing child who'd fuss and refuse to drink formula all night, of her mother-in-law who, with her own sleepless nights of child-rearing behind her, might scold or even shake the little girl, and not even waiting for the other women who were leaving the village, made her way through the middle of the field, skirting the barbed wire–enclosed towers of the border guards, and set off. As her path cut through the sparse grove, she quickened her steps to reach the river shallows. Right then, her phone rang, blending with her heavy breathing and the crunch of soil underfoot, as just above all these borders, homelands, and walls separating people, birds *ch-reeed* to its tune. She heard her mother: "Have you crossed yet, daughter? Is O'ngar's house open?" Zarina had left late in the afternoon after hours spent sitting and laughing with her mother and siblings. Her brother had driven her part of the way from the village and left her near the end of the road—no one dared go farther, since people snuck across the border there for all kinds of reasons, and bullets were often flying. For men especially it was dangerous to wander near the border in these parts. Because of the approaching dusk and the long road, her family worried about her. Although Zarina had grown up playing in these vast and deserted fields, although she could retrace her steps and reach the village in five minutes if she wanted, the night's closeness and the fact that lately she'd seen suspicious people in uniforms and civilian clothes here with cold expressions on their faces put her on edge and made her wary. Noises carried from the village on the evening wind: the agitated bleating of calves for their mothers, the distant sputtering of tractors, and the squawking of chickens fighting for a spot in some faraway yard. Under her feet, leaves and shriveled fruit—last year's apricots and apples—rustled and crunched. Ten or eleven years ago this land had been the aul's largest grove, but now it could hardly be called a grove at all. When the border was drawn it had been left between the two countries, neutral ground that was neglected and overgrown. It was as though the trees and wildflowers had swallowed whole her childhood laughter and excitement beneath the endless sky and the still-warm embers of first love. As though, if she kept walking, some neighbor boys and girls might jump out from behind a hill or tree and shout "boo!" In late autumn, the grove took on a golden hue, then turned red, before everything was blanketed in snow, and she remembered herding sheep with the other children, driving cows, playing, walking, and the bitter smell of burning leaves.

The dense woods rustled as, from the birds' nests hanging like little turbans from the branches and buzzing in the wind, all kinds of black birds soared out at once, vanishing into the darkness. Then, through the overgrown branches skimming the ground, from beneath the apple and peach trees, as though bubbling from the earth, a forlorn crowd of loose-haired women appeared like some enchanted army. Zarina's legs stiffened, refusing to go any farther. At the head of the crowd walked an elderly woman, seemingly its leader. Leaning on a staff, yet upright and spry—her head wrapped in a large white scarf, and a whispered, half-swallowed prayer of "bismillah..." issuing from her toothless lips in time with her steps—she had eyes that, like her body, were ancient, sunken, and waning. But there was a hardness and suffering in the eyes of this katxudo-momo so that, without even swinging her cane, she could command the younger women behind her, urging them on as though with her mind. Next to her, Marina, round-faced and bareheaded, her bleached blonde hair untidy, looked about frantically with her black eyes, speaking as though to herself, spit flying from her mouth. "Ibi-yay! Voy! Don't jump! I told her. Stop! I said. There were some people out fighting with Eldor again on the street. Then that idiot Dilsanam threw herself out the window saying, I can't go on living with Eldor. My heart came crashing and tearing down with her. I saw her body lying on the ground from the seventh floor. She looked like a crumpled tulip or a flag blown down by the wind. Crumpled tulips everywhere. Then I laughed and cried. Tears of blood flowed from my mother and father's eyes when they saw me. I was forced to go to a place for crazy women, old crones with tangled hair, and numb girls. A woman in white gave me a shot every day. At the beginning, I'd yell, No, don't. But the others, those butchers, would slap and hit me saying, Lie down and take it, lard-ass, you're better off. Slowly I got used to it, and no longer bothered to fight. At night I was visited by all kinds of men. That's a movie, Marina, the people you see on TV visit your dreams at night, said the white-robed woman. I kept having the dreams. What didn't they do to me in that madhouse? They put a child in my womb. The woman in white says I'm pregnant by a guy from the movies. Could that be?"

As if to prove it, the delinquent wind flattened the girl's shirt against her bulging belly. Zarina stepped aside as the women started shouting. Out of the crowd stepped a middle-aged woman. "Girls, ladies, eat some xonim, it's getting cold.

You haven't tasted salt for a week," she said, circling the procession with a plate. Other ferocious women put her in her place: "Get lost! Take your xonim and shove it!"

In tight pants, with large breasts spilling from a low-cut shirt, her face painted red and blue, a long blonde ponytail tied high on her head, Albina addressed the blue-eyed Russian woman next to her: "I said to my husband, Are you even a man? Don't you know how I earn the money I bring home so the children can eat? He scowled and said no. But he knew where I went at night. In the morning when he saw the money he knew exactly where I'd been. Because sometimes the drunken men would go into a rage and bite my fat or pummel my body, neck, and chest, covering me in bruises."

Zarina's steps slowed as she watched the women. The early evening birdsong and the gurgling of nearby waters quieted. With the sun's last rays, the leaves on the trees, the flowers in the fields, and even the soil turned red. The older women walked with a ghostly step, pleading woefully with God, while the younger ones in the middle of the procession, girls with frozen pupils, walked as though their minds were elsewhere, and only their feet were carrying them forward. From time to time, one girl would step out from the end of the row, stand on a stump, and recite a poem:

From the wine I took a sip.
I drank your blood,
But whose blood
I wonder,
Did you drink, grape?

The katxudo-momo in the white headscarf furrowed her brow as if to tell the poetess, "Stop dreaming and get in line." But since she was just a child, she kept reciting her poetry and humming folk melodies under her breath.

At the edge of the crowd, a young woman holding a white baby blanket slowed a little as though recognizing Zarina. "Sister, where are you coming from?" Zarina pictured O'ngaraka's yard with its gate on the village side of the border and garden in the neighboring country, and all the people who gathered on his supa, waiting for the guards to pass by so they could sneak across. According to her brothers, livestock grazing near the border often went missing, and the previous winter two young shepherds who'd gone out in search of their horses had also disappeared without a trace. Uphill from the grove, not far from the main road, was a path that led to O'ngar's yard. Zarina used to swim across the border but had twice fallen ill after the journey. "Don't go that way again, sister," her brother had scolded her. "Are you trying to blow out your lungs? Just get your papers in order." To cross at the official checkpoint required all kinds of documents and a fee. The locals who'd been living here for years, giving their daughters away and taking brides across the border, would crawl beneath barbed wire and wade through water to avoid it. Zarina began to cross instead through O'ngar-aka's yard. Everyone knew her there, and if she was late in arriving or wasn't seen for a week, they'd call her up: "Zarina-xon, where've you been, everything all right?" O'ngar-aka's wife knew that she was nursing and would cook pots of food every time Zarina came through—she'd care for her, like any mother. Zarina paid nothing for these kindnesses. She had no money—this was why she couldn't cross at central customs. She was too shy to accept money from her family, but her mother always managed to slip some in her pocket. So she replied "yes" when her brother asked, "Do you have any money?" while still hoping he'd insist, and when he didn't, she felt hurt and cried all alone on the road. "No matter what happens, your husband is our relative and you'll be happy with him. We'll support each other," her brother had said when she was married off to a relative. Her husband Rustamjon was a good man and took care of her. But there was some chink in the girl's heart, and maybe that was why, each month, she crossed the border three or four times to see her mother.

The girl collected herself and stared at the departing crowd. Who were they? Where were they going at this hour? Or was this all some tragic hallucination? She placed her hands on her chest to calm her heartbeat and recited the prayers and verses she knew from memory. The cool evening air drew the scent of wild herbs and dew to her nose. She sneezed from the cold. On the horizon, the golden colors of dusk stood out, signaling the approaching darkness. The chipping trill of sparrows and Afghan starlings rose above the reddening oleasters at the edge of the grove. The old woman at the head of the procession said, "You come, too. We also are of you," as though reciting a prayer. Her white hair blew lifelessly in the wind. "I have a nursing child, mother," Zarina said. "I've got to get home or she'll cry herself blue. I refused my own mother when she asked me to sit a while and have some dinner. What's the matter with me, now, I'm wandering lost."

She watched the crowd as they silently proceeded, then, dressed in black, long hair flowing, the strange women came to a stop before following the katxudo-momo back into the grove. Night's falling, what path do they mean to take? Zarina wondered. They must not know the country well. "There's no path that way, sisters," she said. The loose-haired women, still pleading with God, continued slowly, slowly, into the heart of the grove. She heard the lamentations of the older women—"Voy! My soul, my dear, dear child!"—and of the young women and girls—"My hero! Sweetheart." A bareheaded woman with disheveled hair was wearing a military uniform with the shoulder straps torn off and, despite being about thirty or thirty-five, was bent over by some undisclosed grief, her face pale as an inmate chained up in a dark prison for a hundred years. With every step, she gritted her teeth and cursed in Uzbek and Russian, "Anvar, you bastard, come out! I'll teach you. A wife's not enough, huh, you go chasing after young girls?" The women's mournful faces, the brushwood stuck to their wet hair, and their frozen pupils struck horror in Zarina's heart.

Hurrying on, Zarina returned to her senses. She glanced back and saw that the crowd had already disappeared into the grove. Must have been women from a neighboring aul gathering after a tragedy or for a funeral, she thought.

As usual, by the time she'd reached the hill and the barbed wire fence that would guide her toward O'ngar's house, she was sweating heavily and out of breath. She took a handkerchief from the pocket of the wool jacket she wore over her red dress and wiped her nose. Her throat burned from running such a long way. She raised her head and looked anxiously at the darkening horizon. A cry of "My chiiild" rose within her. Just then, two men in border guard uniforms appeared, as though from the sky. Zarina was about to throw herself backward into the thicket when she heard a machine gun's rattle.

"Stop! Who are you? What's your name?"

"Zarina... Ova."

A fountain of flames rose within her, blocking her throat.

"Where are you going?"

"I lost my cows. I'm looking for them."

"Don't lie, Citizen Zarina. You're breaking the law. This is a border area. Trespassing is prohibited."

Seeing she wouldn't be able to lie her way out of the situation, she started to beg:

"I'm going home, brothers. Through O'ngar-aka's... I left late, and I have a nursing baby... My other children are alone... Please..."

"You're coming to the station, Citizen Zarina. You'll answer to the authorities."

"Take pity on me. My mother lives in one of the mountain auls, and I live across the border. Let me go, brothers. Or my baby won't sleep tonight."

"Come down from there, Citizen Zarina. Stop wasting our time."

Seeing the border guards start to crawl up the hill, Zarina threw herself backward into the thicket. Rolling down the slope, her neck, shoulders, legs, and face were struck, scraped, skinned, crimsoned by crunching brushwood and stones, her speed increasing until she landed with a splash in the rushing water at the mouth of a large pipe. The girl's whole body trembled from fear and cold as, not stopping to think, she dove into the pipe, whose mouth was larger than a man's body. The water was flowing from somewhere near O'ngar-aka's yard, she understood. For a few moments, she was pushed under by the current and thought she would drown, but then, thrashing, she got her head above the surface. Her throat and nose stung from gulping the water. The tat-tat of the border guards' machine guns and their cries of "Hey, you, stop, stop!" were still audible. A terrible thought stuck in her mind: I told them my name, and now they'll certainly come after me. Suddenly, the face of one of the loose-haired women returned to her and she remembered they'd studied together at school. But senseless from the cold, she couldn't remember the girl's name. Along with the water flowing into her nose, she'd been struck by a venomous chill. Her whole body shivered. She struggled onward, bracing her hands and feet against the walls of the pipe. But because they were coated with some kind of slime, her limbs would slip, and she'd be pushed back a few meters, her head and body hitting the walls. The upper part of the pipe was blocked off by brushwood and clothing—other women smuggling goods across the border had waded through the pipe before, and their clothing had gotten snagged. They too used secret routes to avoid paying at the checkpoint. Zarina hurried on as though the guards were chasing her. She pushed and pulled the branches aside, mouth open and gasping convulsively for air. Her pleas of "God have mercy on my child, deliver me from misfortune, my God, let me see my child again" echoed through the pipe. Just when Zarina thought she might suffocate, she caught sight of the end of the pipe, but the ceiling was low and the water high, and even if she swam underwater, even if she made it to the end, the opening might be blocked by a grate or something else, and she might never get out. It seemed certain she'd die. She trembled with fear and despair. "Here goes." Tears poured from her eyes as, pleading with God, she dove underwater. She groped with her cold-stiffened hands trying to grasp the end of the pipe, then—pop—she was back outside. The mouth of the pipe was open. Like a mythical pari who'd lived a hundred years beneath the water, Zarina came up splashing. Her dress and hair floated on the water's surface. Her jacket had gotten snared somewhere back in the pipe. Too weak now for caution, she was no longer mainly concerned with crossing the border, but with surviving. Gasping, she clung with all her might to the branches and twigs at the edge of the canal, clambering up the bank so as not to slip back into the swirling currents of the pipe. She was overtaken, body and soul, by the joyful message "I'm saved." Shuddering from the cold, she crawled, dragging herself, to a tree near the water's edge and collapsed, breathing heavily. Water streamed from her hair, and she shook from head to toe in her soaked clothing. Night had fallen, and she couldn't make out her surroundings. A dirty white piece of sky shone dimly through the treetops, but her teeth chattered, and no clear thought came to her mind. Suddenly, a wool shawl was thrown over her and Zarina looked up, glaring. She saw the long-haired girl, her classmate whose name she couldn't remember, and then the other loose-haired women from the other side. "I've just recognized you, Farog'at, assalom," Zarina said in a whisper. "Womankind helps its own, in this world and the next," her classmate said slowly. Then Zarina heard music and laughter. The group sat in a circle around a great bonfire while a woman with a kerchief tied at an angle on her head, brows darkened with osma, sang. In the middle, crazy Marina and the soft-hearted, voluptuous prostitute Albina danced, though their faces remained stern, and the woman in a service uniform marched in military style—clomp, stomp—while everyone around cheered "hayit, hayit!" A woman slapped and rattled the childirma, urging the dancers on even more, shouting "Hop-hop!" and "Come, come on!"

Then the katxudo-momo directed the dark crowd to continue on its way. Zarina stood dumbfounded watching them with a cup of hot tea in her hand. The young woman Farog'at flashed her a broken smile. "Won't you walk with us, Zarina-xon?" "I have a nursing child at home, I'm headed to O'ngaraka's yard," Zarina said. Suddenly everyone stopped what they were doing and the mad, healthy, crippled, and injured women went off, crowing and chortling: "You haven't crossed over yet, you're still wandering lost like us." The crazy woman danced toward her. "For six months we've been wandering between two worlds. What gives you the right to cross?" she said. "Don't you know the earth is round, you blockhead?" said the soldier woman. The crazy woman, the voluptuous prostitute, and the soldier woman leapt and twirled at the head of the procession. The poetess, with her two long braids, climbed atop a stump:

Now I have no right to die,
Gloomy nights I made fly
From the sad heart's chamber
Like the sun touched by a tree
I'll kiss life's eye.

Then, with a poke of the katxudo-momo's stick, the girl jumped down. "All right, all right," she said, and continued in search of the next stump.

Zarina looked around awestruck, and only then did the *peep-trip-treee* of birds reach her ears, only then did she notice the oleaster looming in the darkness. It was as though the evening had been paralyzed, unable to abide by time's eternal laws.

The dark crowd continued on its way, singing: "My black locks have grown, o'er my brow they fall free, oh what bad business has befallen me..."

Thórdís Helgadóttir

Translated from Icelandic
by Larissa Kyzer

Thórdís Helgadóttir
Sker
Translated from Icelandic
by Larissa Kyzer

The Skerry

Pabbi brought me a live bird. Fat and strong. I know he went to a lot of trouble to get it here. He lashed the bird's legs together and used netting to bind its wings tight to its body. He probably had to tie its beak shut, too, so the men wouldn't go crazy listening to it squawk nonstop at close range. A twelve-hour row on a calm sea. I don't know if it was one of those pink June nights or if the skies were gray and drizzly overhead. But I know it was dead calm, because Pabbi never rows out unless it's dead calm.

I know the men were exhausted and the summer night never-ending. I imagine my bird, lying among the cooling carcasses of its brothers and sisters in the bottom of the boat. It sees nothing but sky. Boot-clad feet do their best not to trample the catch, but there's very little elbow room in the tightly packed clinker boat. The bird must have struggled, at least for the first few hours, and that would have jostled the boat—not a risk-free prospect. I know that. I know that Pabbi went through a lot, put the others through a lot, to bring me the bird. I know that without needing Mamma to remind me.

We were the exact same height, my bird and I, when Pabbi first brought it to me, and this delighted me beyond measure. It was young, its feathers still streaked with gray, clumsy but indefatigable, as if wind and weather didn't affect it at all. At first, we kept it in the hayfield, since it, like the sheep, couldn't get over the low fence. Mamma's never even considered letting the bird in the house, says it's grungy, and I can't argue with her on that. My bird does not smell what you might call good. Mamma wasn't happy that Pabbi gave it to me, but instead of complaining to Pabbi, she seems mad at me.

My sister explained everything to me: The price fetched for the hide of a single bird was enough to keep a whole family in bread for an entire month. The down is in high demand, the skin tough as bull leather. And that's not even counting the meat.

Now the bird follows me wherever I go, waddling after me through gardens and lava fields. It's slow, but surefooted. I filch scraps of hardfish and suet to slip to it, and over time it's grown quite attached to me. It'll never come around to Pabbi, though, and Mamma and it look through one another like ghosts.

Some of the other kids have their own birds, too. Usually, they're kept tied to stakes in the hayfields, but sometimes we play with them. We take them on walks, dress them up, crown them with flower wreaths, marry them to one another. But they don't seem particularly given to marriages of convenience and, unless they're just really good at hiding them, the birds never lay any eggs.

Which is a real shame. Because those eggs would fetch a good price. I know several natural history museums have promised Pabbi the sun, moon, and stars, but the men never snatch eggs. They wait until mid-June to row out to the skerry. That way, they can be sure that all the eggs have hatched and the young are out of the nest. Even if the hunting is much harder as a result. While the birds are still brooding, they're slow and reluctant to venture too far from their eggs; it would be easy to run them down. After their eggs hatch, though, they spend more time in the sea. Pabbi says they dive off cliffs, quick as a flash, plunge majestically into the waves, and then waddle back onto the rocky shore with beakfuls of sand lance.

We mustn't forget our duty, says Pabbi. The stock is fragile, we know that. You can see it in a lot of places around the island, places where the bird was common years back, now you don't hardly see it anymore. They say that in neighboring countries, the species has entirely vanished. It's in everyone's best interest that we act with prudence and moderation. We really can't do otherwise.

The men row out to the skerry. The women tan the hides. There aren't many of us here in the fjord—six families. Only landowners have hunting rights. I don't know how anyone else would do it anyway. It's only us, the people of the fjord, who know the way out.

Most summers, we get visiting naturalists here, some from abroad. Pabbi lends them boats and men and maps. But they almost never make it out. The sea's too rough and so they sit frowning in our parlor at home, waiting for their chance. I let them examine my bird as long as I'm there when they do. I stroke it between the eyes while the scientists poke its short wings or feed it. Sometimes, they want to observe it for long stretches of time, and they talk to me as they do, in English and Danish, which eventually, I start to understand. But there always comes the point when they lose patience. When that happens, they either go home, hopes dashed, or decide the time is now, no matter what Pabbi says, that this is good enough, and out they row. A few hours later, dark clouds roll across the sky, and they turn around, terrified and storm-tossed. Then they get sick, and Mamma tucks them into bed and spoon-feeds them soup.

Hen soup, she says. But they can see, of course, that the meat is black and some of them won't eat it. But the ones who do always recover quicker.

Hunting hasn't been good this year. There has been only one other voyage this summer and they caught only three birds. One man drowned—the oldest son of the farmer who lives all the way at the base of the fjord. It's always a risk, even in good weather. The voyage is twelve hours in an open, eight-oared boat. Some men are completely sapped by the time they come home and are forced to spend the next few days in bed. Others drown.

Mamma doesn't sleep before or during a voyage to the skerry. The night before, she prepares provisions. Might as well, she'll be awake all night anyway. At daybreak, when the men set out, she sits down with her knitting. Other work can wait. It's like she believes that the men will stay alive only as long as her needles are still clacking away. I'm careful not to bother her, keep out-of-doors, scale the cliffs, climb boulders and hills, eat sheep sorrel late into the bright night. Mamma doesn't utter a word when I'm finally tired enough to creep in with grass-green soles, dizzy from hunger and fresh air. On these nights, I'm a wildling, thinking thoughts that would otherwise never occur to me.

I wake to a commotion outside, and I know the boat's been spotted. Mamma's bustling around the kitchen, heating up coffee and boiled fish. A freshly knitted sweater is folded atop the dresser. I hurry outside and take my bird behind the house before they bring the catch into the yard. I don't want it to see the carcasses.

They have only one bird this time. There's suddenly a wariness about them, says Pabbi. Not that there aren't plenty of birds on the skerry, thank goodness. They're just so terribly guarded. Mamma purses her lips. In the coming days, she'll neither sew nor knit; instead, she'll weave nets, breathable garments for winter-hardy beasts.

But all the men came back this time. Men who can't swim sailing after birds that can't fly. There's a certain justice to it. Not that anyone would ever state it outright.

We kids gather later that day. Some bring their birds; most are in low spirits. The families who live deepest in the fjord have been talking about abandoning their farms. The sheep have been dying and now the hunting is going poorly. Pabbi says they don't know how to read the waters.

One of the younger boys bursts into tears. His face goes gray, he can't speak for sobbing, and then he runs off up the mountainside. A few days later, we figure out why when his pabbi drives to town with bird hide and meat to sell. His bird was the biggest of all, young and fat and the only one that could keep up with us when we ran.

My sister keeps watch for me that night. We know how this goes, she says. There's only one way this ends. I hem and haw. We're not so bad off, I say. Pabbi works harder than anyone; he's the best hunter by far. And we have fewer mouths to feed than the others. And fewer hands to help, she says. What if they stop hunting on the skerry altogether?

There's a painting hanging in the parlor. A big, serious painting that Pabbi had sent over from England. It was painted from a drawing one of the naturalists made based on an account of Pabbi's one rainy summer. In the painting, though, it's sunny. Somehow, the big skerry has been drawn correctly, but the directions are all wrong. Five strapping men have come ashore. They look like important men, well-groomed and handsome. One is grappling with a bird of some size; two others are dragging a carcass out to their boat. In the foreground, eggs lie in an abandoned nest. That's simultaneously the truest and falsest thing about the picture, says Pabbi. The painter had real specimens in an English natural history museum to work from. But we'd never kill a bird that was still brooding.

I often imagine what my bird would think of this painting if I ever let it in the house. Would it recognize itself? Would it mistake it for real and try to protect the eggs?

I've never tied the bird up. It's happened before that it's waddled down to the shore behind me when I've forgotten it was there. But it never dives into the sea, just shuffles its feet uncertainly on the sand and nibbles on seaweed or stands there gazing out over the fjord. It seems sad to me in these moments. I wait awhile and then lure it back with pieces of blood pudding. It eats anything it's given; our leftovers and scraps usually end up in its trough. But I'm sure it craves fresh, wriggling fish.

The summer passes without any more voyages out to the skerry. The weather is mild, but Pabbi says the wind is blowing from an unfavorable direction and the current will be stronger farther out. Fortunately, the fishing has been good for everyone. Mamma is awake late into the night and never seems to have a free moment. She says it's time for me to contribute and stop doing everything according to my own personal preferences. She makes me rake and do the washing and seems mad at me even though I do everything she says, as if she suspects I want to shirk my responsibilities. But I don't want to shirk my responsibilities. I even ask if I can do more, if I can help with the mending, for instance, but she just snorts, wrinkles her nose, and says I'm not allowed anywhere near a piece of cloth so long as I smell like a bird cliff. I get a lump in my throat when she says that. Long to run away to some bird cliff somewhere for real. Live on a ledge with my bird and do everything according to my own personal preferences. I can do way more than my mom realizes. I can do everything I want.

Then, one day, the summer is over. There's a bite in the air. The men are unhappy. Some want to make a final attempt to row out to the skerry before the winter takes hold. Pabbi says it's no use. Someone gets mad and says Pabbi doesn't have as much at stake. He tells them to go ahead and row out without him. Everyone is standoffish the next day. Soon, it will be time for the sheep roundup. As far back as I remember, the people in this fjord have harped on about getting along to go along, said unity is an absolute prerequisite for thriving here. We have to be in lockstep, they say, hand in hand. Anything else and the community doesn't stand a chance.

One night, my sister wakes me before daybreak.

Now, she says.

Are you sure? I ask, but my sister is always sure.

I pull my bag out of the recess behind the headboard where I hid it. I've had everything ready for a long time. I tiptoe into the kitchen to get some provisions. I would have loved to bring a thermos of hot coffee like the men do, but Mamma is a light sleeper, and the sound of the coffee mill might wake her. So I stuff some food in a bag, get the bird, and row out.

Rowing is hard work, even when the sea is still. The boat is too big, and the oars get tangled in the cordage. After an hour, my shoulders ache so much I have to rest. The bird squirms and squawks loudly. It doesn't like being tied up. I see the way it's looking out at the sea, following the movements of the shorebirds with its eyes. Maybe it's looking for its family. Eventually, it falls silent, hoarse and hopeless, and we both nod off.

It's afternoon when I wake, and the weather has turned cold. It's September. I cast out, and before long I have a sculpin on the line. I give it to the bird and eat a slice of mutton headcheese from my bag. The bird perks up when I feed it, nearly swallows my hand in its gluttony. Once we've both eaten our fill, I loosen its bonds. Without a moment's hesitation, my bird clambers up on the gunwale and dives into the sea.

I don't know how far we are from the skerry. We've undoubtedly floated off course while I was sleeping. But the bird seems to have a good sense of direction. It heads east, and I follow.

This isn't what I intended to do. I'd planned to turn around once I'd released it. See my bird's home and then scram back to the village to be scolded within an inch of my life. But then all of a sudden it took off and I didn't even have a chance to say goodbye.

I row after the bird for a long time. It's happy, diving now and then to fish. I've never seen it so lively or agile. On land, it's sluggish and its wings are of no use to it for flying; it's clearly made for water.

Darkness falls and I can no longer see it. Even so, I keep rowing in the direction I think is east. Just a bit farther. I'm rested and my stomach is full. I'm feeling fine.

My sister comes and sits beside me in the dark. Look how the sky and the sea run together, she says. This is what it's like to be out in space.

How out in space? I ask, but she doesn't answer.

I don't know how long I've been rowing blind. I don't think I'm ever going to find the skerry, I tell my sister.

You're here, she answers.

And a second later, the boat slams into rock. I pull it up onto the shore, crawl into the bottom, and wrap myself up in a thick blanket it took Mamma weeks to crochet.

All the other kids have siblings. On most farms, there are five kids, maybe more. One of the older girls told me Mamma almost died when she had me. Something inside her was damaged and so she can't have any more kids. My sister has been with me ever since I can remember. For a long time, it didn't occur to me to ask why she didn't have her own bed or why she never ate with us at mealtime. Mamma and Pabbi never mentioned her and so I never brought her up with them, either. And so when I wanted to ask, it took me a long time to work up the courage.

Are you a ghost?

Most families have lost children. The plots are close-set in the churchyard; there are specters in all the houses. Little is said about the babes who never make it out of the nest. Maybe my sister died at birth. Maybe I got her name.

She frowns.

Me? she asks. Why would I be a ghost? Maybe you're a ghost.

I don't ask again after that. I'm not too keen on the idea that I could be a ghost. I think I would know it if I were a ghost. A person ought to know if they're a ghost.

I wake to the sound of rain and a guttural, gargling cacophony. The drizzle has soaked through the blanket and I'm cold. The day is bright, and the sun is high in the sky, peeking out from behind the fast-moving clouds. There are squawking birds on all sides. My sister is gone.

I stand up and grope for my bag of food. My body is stiff, and my hands are numb with cold. It takes me a long time to loosen the knot, a long time to chew. The flatbread has dried up and the whey cheese is hard. I walk around to warm myself up as I eat, pace back and forth on the shore while the Arctic terns glide overhead.

The birds are farther inland. They're waiting in a grassy hollow and don't run away from me, but they also don't venture any closer. I've never seen so many of them all at once. There must be dozens. Some are little and gray, still chicks. The white patches on their temples are like pupilless eyes, and I have the feeling that they are watching every move I make from beyond, another plane almost. I try to pick out my bird in the crowd, but truth be told, I'm not sure I'd be able to tell it apart from the others.

And maybe it's not even here. This isn't the skerry, I realize right away and not just because I'd recognize it from the painting and Pabbi's descriptions. These are lowlands. The shore slopes gently and I trudge across sand dunes, push through tall, grayish reeds. The clouds hang low in the heavens, the sky behind them cold and blue. The birds scatter as I approach, waddle away as if suddenly remembering an urgent errand they have to take care of.

Leaving the shore, I come to a dell. Little knolls block out the horizon. If this is an island, it's a big one. Bigger than the islands that lie out beyond our fjord. I must have drifted a long way off course. I wish my sister were here.

A flock of birds are milling about around a brook in the deepest part of the dell, grazing on the grass like sheep in an inverted world. A little girl is in the stream, bedheaded and barefooted, wading. She can't be older than six. There must be a farm nearby. I'm sure I've never seen this girl before. But I feel like I know her all the same.

I take pains not to frighten the girl as I approach. The birds splash and scuttle across the stream, keeping ten to twenty meters between themselves and me. When the girl looks up, I flash her my meekest expression. I'm prepared for her to jump, maybe even get scared and run away. But then a smile crosses her face. She runs to me and throws herself into my arms. I hug her tight. Her hair is redolent of outdoor air and dulse, the hollow of her neck scented salty and woody and more wonderful than anything I've smelled in my entire life. I love her immediately.

She calls her bird over to show me. It comes, tame, butting its head into my waist. I comb the girl's hair, call her a wildling. She laughs. She has a den in a cavern where she cuddles up with the bird every night. It brings her fish, and when she's hungry enough, she eats it raw.

I give the girl headcheese and boiled rutabagas. At night, when she falls asleep, I gently pry myself from her arms and hurry up the highest hillock before the light completely fades. In day's waning glow, I look out across the landscape. The fall colors are soft and warm, but my breath becomes a frosty column in the cold night air. To the east, beyond the hillocks, ever-taller pillars of lava obscure the horizon. To the west, the blue sea meets the sky and nothing stands between them.

When I turn around to go back down the slope, I see her bird standing there at a distance. As soon as I look at it, it starts carefully picking its way down the rocky scree on its little legs, as if to let me know I don't concern it in the slightest.

It was just a coincidence that it was passing by. It would never occur to it to follow me.

There was a freeze overnight. The girl wakes up with a runny nose. I wrap the blanket around her, and she gradually stops shivering.

I try to be as nice as possible. I gather driftwood on the shore, and the girl gets a kick out of that. I ask her to help me. She collects stones and moss while I build something akin to skeletons out of the branches. Then we fill them in, put meat on their bones. The birds stand nearby preening themselves. Now and then, one leaps off the cliff and into the foaming sea. They seem immune to the cold.

When we're done, we collect straw and use it to cover the figures.

See? I say to my little sister. That's their skin.

She nods.

The bird is fat, she says.

Sure is, I say. And the girl?

She looks at the slender little figure that's supposed to represent her. Then at the straw bird. And shakes her head.

I motion for her to hand me a feather that's lying in the sand. I dip it deep into the fizzy sea and give it a shake.

My little sister feels it with her fingertips and her eyes become saucers:

It's dry.

She refuses to leave the seashore until we've feathered the bird figure from head to tail. I figure out how to string the feathers together with thick blades of fescue grass and she copies me. Around noon, we sit down and eat what's left of the food I brought. The birds have gotten bored with us and wandered off. All but one, which stands at a distance, barely visible against the gray-wet, rocky shoreline. It's staring motionless in the opposite direction, upland. My sister snuffles.

The next time I look up, the bird is fully feathered. The girl has snuck a few feathers into her hair and under her collar.

Later, in the boat, she cries. I don't try to comfort her, that's not my job. She gets to cry for what she's lost. My job is to shoulder responsibility. To tear her away from what she loves so that both she and it will live.

At first, she wants to help me row, but her scrawny arms tire quickly. Instead, she gets to have my blanket and to sleep in the bottom of the boat with a fishy-smelling feather clenched in her fist.

As the night wears on, I get pins and needles in my arms. My shoulders stiffen and the pain's unbearable, but still I row. I can do everything I want.

I get us to land through obstinance alone. My little sister is cold, but tranquil and well-rested; I'm soaked to the bone and completely spent. I wake her a bit brusquely.

Go on now.

You aren't coming with me? she asks with nothing but her eyes.

We'll see, I say.

I watch her go in the early morning light. The wet sand on the beach swallows her little feet and she has to yank them up and out with each step. The wind is in her face as she goes to receive my scolding, dragging my blanket behind her.

A few years later, her dell will be found again. A remote bay one fjord over where no one lives, accessible only by sea. Of the hoards that once were, only ten sickly birds remain. No chicks, no stone bird on the beach. The men take all of them. The catch saves five farms from a hunger winter, but people know better than to tempt fate. No one's expecting any miracles, and in the spring, the farms are all abandoned. The farmers split the proceeds from the sale of the bird pelts and the people start new lives elsewhere. Paltry lives, perhaps, but still better than desperately lapping death from mussel shells.

Pabbi becomes withdrawn, gets a faraway look in his eyes whenever the birds are mentioned. He doubtless suspects that those were the last ones, long before any accusations are publicly made. He refuses to talk about it for the rest of his life—even when he's mentioned by name, even when the other men come forward to defend their honor and demand he stand with them. He says he can't be dwelling on the past; leather and soles are all he thinks about now. But it's clear that his talents do not lie in repairing shoes. Life in his new profession will always be a damnable grind. Mamma, on the other hand, is making decent money as a seamstress, and together they eke out a new life in a real town.

My sister helps out. Over time, she settles down, quits capering about like a wildling, and Mamma gradually softens toward her child. Besides, my sister is my mother's equal when it comes to work—she's quick to learn and never complains. The years pass. With age, the elder woman's temperament hardens anew, and she directs her foul moods at her daughter, who always has her own ideas about material and patterns and, with her sharp eye and steady hand, has long since eclipsed her mother as a seamstress.

Miraculously, they manage to scrounge up enough money after a few years to open their own tailor shop. My sister buys a big, stately building in the center of town and hires a girl to be her assistant. When Mamma's hands are finally claimed by rheumatism, my sister takes over the running of the shop alone. The change is visible in the garments. The lace trim on dress sleeves and collars is more delicate than before. The silk is specially imported from England, and skillfully constructed corsets transform the town's gentlewomen into knockouts overnight.

My sister is industrious, talented, and uniquely discerning. She can sniff out fashion trends the moment the first whiff blows across the sea. She has a sixth sense for business. She becomes sought-after, then indispensable. She is the first in her family to have money.

She's considered eccentric, sends off for masses of foreign magazines and periodicals, everything from *Myra's Journal of Dress and Fashion* to *Archiv für Naturgeschichte*. She even spends some time sailing around the world. She never marries—but it doesn't follow that her life is loveless. Let's just say she selects her shopgirls with considerable care. She moves out of the apartment above the shop and into an elegant new house with a big back garden where she plants flowering hedges and herbs and keeps chickens. She keeps her private life private, and shares nothing of her loves nor of her troubles and heartbreaks. She buries her parents a few years apart, both with great dignity.

When rheumatism, that hereditary scourge, settles into her joints, she's done well enough for herself that it doesn't really matter. Her brain still works, and she's trained the girls well. From then on, she keeps an eagle eye on the management and visits her lady customers no less frequently than before, the better to assure them they won't get anything as fashionable or as skillfully made anywhere in town.

She stands so tall and upright, this sister of mine, shows almost no indication of ever walking into a headwind. She maintains her posture in all weather, even when fortune turns against her. One fateful November day, she's cheated in both love and business. The woman who has lived under her roof for many years—tenant, friend, shopgirl, beloved—moves out and opens her own tailor, in direct competition with my sister. With her, she takes customers, employees, and know-how. She steals business relationships at home and abroad. Spreads malicious rumors.

It's a heavy blow, but not heavy enough to fell my sister. She wakes up the next morning and announces that she'll be closing shop. Then she calmly and methodically gets to work tying up loose ends—tight and firm, so they won't come undone again. This done, she's carefree and easy; she's amassed quite a sum that will make her old age bearable, a cherry atop a life well-lived.

That's when the insomnia sets in. Her soul's uneasy. The idleness of her twilight years dredges up what was lurking beneath the surface. She can't concentrate on reading or writing. The house is both a vast expanse and a prison cell. Neither the pharmacist nor priest can offer her any relief.

Then she receives a letter from Copenhagen. From a good friend of hers, a beautiful man with a pianist's fingers from whom she sourced delicate lacework for decades. He tells her of the medical practice of hypnotizing a patient back into their past. He knows of a doctor with a gift for ferreting out the peas of youth buried under hundreds of mattresses so a troubled soul might rest easy in its skin once more.

My sister cannot recall having ever put any faith in the great beyond or sorcery of any kind. But her friend assures her that, quite to the contrary, this is science—neither more nor less than the best, most cutting-edge science of the modern day: the science of the soul.

And so she sets out on another journey. Sails to Copenhagen, and from there onward to Hamburg and Frankfurt. On the way, she visits natural history museums, wandering their corridors and seeking out halls in which the speckled eggs of extinct birds are safeguarded under glass. She recognizes a few. When she finally reaches her destination, Zurich, a solemn young doctor with a black mustache is waiting for her, and she decides to trust this man with her life. She's too old to start doing things by halves.

Under the unwavering guidance of the doctor, she begins a new journey, this time a night sail, inward. And in the dark, she meets a young woman who is also her, an angry woman who she hasn't thought of in years. The woman is standing alone in a world that isn't meant for her, forced into hiding and deceit, into a hard shell, warped by prejudice and disdain.

It's her sister. She can feel the anguish of this young woman, her rage, and forgives her—all her mistakes, all the undeserved severity she rained upon those she loved the most. She spreads a blanket over her, cuddles her close, and rocks her to sleep. She doesn't know anything about the science of the soul, but she understands exactly what this young woman needs to hear, and in her ear, she whispers everything she's learned over her long life.

And when this young woman hears the whispers on the wind, she pushes her own boat out. Charts her course, rows deeper into the night of herself to meet a lonely teenage girl in an unfriendly city. The daily struggle to survive has taken too much from her parents for them to have anything left to give, and so the girl is forced to be her own family.

She is her sister, this teenage girl. She has tamed herself, wrung the wildness out of her being so as not to provoke her mother by simply existing. The mother who, from early childhood, was forced to shoulder responsibilities that would quash any wildling. And now she's empty, alone, living on the margins in a big city. Her father glassy-eyed and bitter, and she doesn't get to mourn him any more than she did the only being she ever loved more.

The young woman whispers and the girl wakes in the night. Sails a tarred rowboat into the innermost darkness and comes out the other side. Makes landfall, walks up to a bare-bottomed child sitting in the sand beside a stone bird. It's her job to comfort this little sister, this self. Who already has everything she needs to survive. Who already knows everything. Who safeguards love deep inside herself and takes it with her wherever she goes.

The little one hears her sister whisper: Your courage is immense. The world is your natural habitat.

And as soon as she hears those words—says those words—the old woman sees her life transposed. Sees how all these women, all her sisters, are one, like different patterns that interweave in one garment. If she sews them together, she'll have a flawless pelt, tailor-made for her alone. And when she puts it on, her heart will finally finally finally be quiet once more.

She thanks the doctor, pays him well. She will sing his praises widely. She makes ready for her journey and leaves Zurich. Maybe she'll stay awhile with her gallant friend in Copenhagen, maybe she'll erect a memorial to her father in the bay. Maybe she'll set sail, collect natural artifacts or lovers.

It is one of those rare moments when everything is as yet undetermined.

The water licks my toes. My feet are wet and my whole body is pins and needles. I've used the last of my energy to drag the clinker ashore. It is now lying athwart on the beach.

The little one has reached the farm, and soon, someone will come out and find her. She's tousled and wild but walks straight into the gusts, unafraid of everything. I whisper on the wind about the nest our bird has hidden at the base of the cliff on the beach. About the three eggs, conceived out of wedlock and abandoned rather than letting them hatch into bondage. Cold and lifeless nest eggs that will safeguard my sister's life and luck. Those eggs will fetch a good price. Like a fairytale princess, she will safeguard them for decades until a little voice in the darkness tells her the time has come.

My big sister is waiting for me farther down the beach. Behind her, I see others. Girls, women. I don't feel like my feet belong to me; I can't feel them touching the ground, but my big sister smiles when I start walking toward her. I walk up to her and into her and out of the fjord. We all walk, onward, the whole way, onward across the water and out to the skerry.

Lusajo Mwaikenda Israel

Translated from Swahili
by Richard Prins

Chakula cha Usiku

Lusajo Mwaikenda Israel

Translated from Swahili
by Richard Prins

Night Meal

It's dawn in the village of Nyangome, the air drizzly and the wind distant. Wema is braiding corn rows in her mother's hair and chatting away. Tunu teases her: "Child, you're a grown woman now. Soon you'll be bringing your mchumba round to ask for your hand." As it happens, Wema's father Mzee Masumbuko is standing in the doorway, listening. He bounds into the conversation. "My dear, don't pester the child. Hurry is worry. She'll find a husband later. Anyway, where can you even find a man to marry these days? The youth are all mixed up on drugs or else drunk." His wife catches herself. "Of course, mume wangu. God's time is the right time." The whole while, Wema just keeps smiling and braiding.

Mzee Masumbuko is a merchant, a pillar of the community, and all the villagers shop at his store. And Wema, let's just say she's his first born as well as last born. Mzee Masumbuko married Tunu, and after a long struggle, making the rounds to several mgangas and drinking all kinds of herbal dawa, they were blessed with just one babe in the hold and named her Wema. Wema was raised with love and tenderness and grew up to be very beautiful, with beer-bottle legs, a hornet's waist, and a neck long as a giraffe's. She took her shape from her mother, which could be why Tunu had just one child. Mzee Masumbuko and his wife visited all the mgangas again, but it was like painting the wind. They never managed to have another.

That night after eating together—for it is Mzee Masumbuko's custom to eat with his family—he calls his wife to their bedroom. "My darling wife, my sweet. Bile of my liver, my breath, I love you dearly." Then he adds, "Please, let me find you a partner, someone to help with your housework and growing our family. Mke wangu, what I mean to say is, one child is no child at all when the government is after her, witches are after her, the whole village is after her. Let me find you a helper, and you can guide her like she's your own sister."

Tunu kneels and weeps like it's the rainy season. Her voice is pure grief when she speaks. "Mume wangu, it is not my wish to be joined by another wife. But since you're my husband, and head of the family, there's no word above yours. Your word is law, and I must accept it."

Mzee Masumbuko's voice becomes low and gentle. "No, my dear. I love you, and I will continue loving you. A junior wife will be your student, and you her elder sister. You will raise her, teach her, and continue to run the household as you like." At these words, Tunu acquiesces, however bent her neck.

Mzee Masumbuko gets another wife. Her name is Kisasi, and she's the daughter of Mzee Kinyambe, a famous mganga who lives in the hills. When Mzee Masumbuko's friends hear he's getting another wife, they advise him not to marry a mganga's daughter. He doesn't listen. For it is true that love is blind, and the lover neither sees nor hears. Mzee Masumbuko weds again with a sumptuous celebration. That day the village is adorned; drums are pounded; cows, goats, chickens, and sheep are devoured. It's a new two-wife life for Mzee Masumbuko.

Mzee Masumbuko continues his custom of eating with his family every evening. The wives take turns preparing dinner. One week his senior wife cooks; the next, his junior wife. Mzee Masumbuko has three houses in his kaya: one for Tunu, one for Kisasi, and another for guests. He takes turns, week by week, sleeping at each of his wives' houses.

Kisasi is not yet pregnant. She makes frequent trips to the mganga for dawa, because it pains her that her co-wife Tunu has a child and she does not. One Sunday, out in the yard in the middle of Mzee Masumbuko's kaya, Tunu and Kisasi hurl sharp words at each other. Kisasi says, "You're witching me so I won't get pregnant. You want me to be just like you, you barren old cow."

Tunu shoots back, "Shut up, you droopy-faced dwarf. Just 'cause your family's a bunch of witches doesn't mean everybody is. You're the barren one; I walk proud with my child. And why's your face look like a used towel in a no-tell motel?"

Kisasi retorts, "Who's the dwarf? I'll kick you like the dog you are." And she charges Tunu, ready to beat her with the pestle she was using to pound kisamvu. Fortunately, Mzee Masumbuko arrives home that moment from the farm. He grabs the pestle just in time.

"Ladies, ladies! Quit it! What is this nonsense?"

As he drags Kisasi toward her house, she sneers, "Little old hag. I'll get you off my back. You'll see."

And Tunu spits back, "See what? And the only hag's your grandma, you filthy hyena."

Two weeks later, Mzee Masumbuko and Kisasi make another trip to the mganga, Kisasi's father Mzee Kinyambe, who gives them an assortment of dawa made from roots, traditional herbs, and tree bark from the forest. By the end of the month, Kisasi is pregnant with twins. She becomes very dear to Mzee Masumbuko. He showers her with presents and sleeps at her house more and more. All this pains Tunu, but she resolves to keep quiet. Hold firm as a bar of soap; cover the bowl till the bastard passes.

Meanwhile, day by day, just as her name says, Kisasi stews revenge in her heart. She plans to pay Tunu back for their quarrel and shut her up.

One night when Kisasi and Mzee Masumbuko are in bed together, she entices him with an idea to give the shop a boost. They can get dawa from a different village this time, far off in the hills, where the archwitch Ndulumi lives. They'll have to take Mzee Masumbuko's motorcycle to get there. He lies to Tunu and says he's going to Mzee Kinyambe's village to fetch more dawa. He leaves Tunu in charge of the shop, which is usually managed by Kisasi.

Archwitch Ndulumi makes her home in a cave filled with bats and spiderwebs, pitch-black except for the frail moonglow leaking through the cracks. As Mzee Masumbuko and Kisasi approach, they hear a deep voice behind them: "Stop where you are. Don't turn around. Squat down. Take off your shoes and come in bowing." That's what they do.

Once inside, they are ordered to take a seat on the hyena skin and close their eyes until told to open them. Archwitch Ndulumi sits on a woven mat with a red blanket around her shoulders. She censes herself with dawa. "I know you want dawa to boost your sales," she announces. "But will you meet my conditions?"

Kisasi says, "Yes, mkuu," and her husband echoes her, "We will, mkuu." So she tells them the first condition is they must make an offering. A child or a wife will do. Kisasi suggests they offer up Tunu, since she can't have any more children, whereas Kisasi can look after the shop and bear him many more twins.

The mganga gives them two different dawas: the first to bathe in the river with, the second to sneak into Tunu's food. After she eats, the mganga explains, she'll feel sick, then die a mysterious, confounding death. They must rush to bury her immediately. But at the burial, they should bury papayas instead, so as to trick the human eye. Then Tunu will turn into a msukule, a bewitched shell of her former self, kept in the shop's storeroom as a charm to attract customers, living off chaff and cassava flour.

And now, a second condition: No one else can ever lay eyes on the msukule. As a precaution, anytime they close the shop, they must keep it closed until the following day, when she's sure to be hidden away. So they go home. Along the way, they pass a river. They take the first enchanted dawa out of its bottle, sealed with red nylon fabric. They rub the yellow powder on their bodies and bathe in the water. The second enchanted dawa is a black liquid in a lidded bottle; that one they bring home. It's Kisasi's turn to cook. She pours the dark fluid over

Tunu's portion; the second it touches the food, it turns invisible. They gather for their night meal.

Tunu eats then goes to bed. Mzee Masumbuko makes sure to retire with his junior wife. As the night passes, Tunu begins to feel very ill. She wakes her daughter for help. Wema gives her medicine for stomach pain and leaves her to rest. For it's true that the ditchdigger must enter the ditch, and when dawn comes, Tunu is even worse off. Wema goes to rouse her father and urge him to rush Tunu to the hospital. Kisasi answers the door.

"She just wants attention, that one. What's she even got?"

Wema charges at her in a fury, but Mzee Masumbuko intervenes. He goes to check on Tunu, knowing in his heart what he has done. She's dead by the time he gets there. The wailing wakes the neighbors.

They take the body to the village hospital for storage. News of her death spreads among relatives, who gather at the home. Though he knows he caused her death, Mzee Masumbuko speaks as the mganga's conditions stipulated: "My wife, while still alive, stated in her will a wish to be buried the same day she died." They stage the burial that afternoon. At the gravesite, Kisasi forces tears and flails her body around on the ground. "Uwiii! Uwiii! Sister, you left me, sister! Who will guide me now? Uwiii!" The tears are a sham. She knows in her heart what she has done, for it is true that a witch has no shame. They spend seven days in mourning, then it's back to business as usual.

Wema works at the woman's salon established by her late mother. One day she gets a call asking her to fill in at the shop. Kisasi has a parents' association meeting at the twins' school. Wema takes care of sales until mid-afternoon, when hunger grabs her like a new mother. She decides to close up shop while she orders something from a nearby cafe. She can eat and wait for Kisasi's return.

For it is true that nothing long is endless. When she reopens the shop later that afternoon, she finds herself face to face with the msukule. She has trouble recognizing the woman who birthed her, given her elongated fingernails, eerily straight hair, and tight skin. She screams; alarmed neighbors come flocking. She faints; they pick her up and carry her to the hospital. The msukule is carted off by Mzee Mbago, chairman of commerce in that section of the market.

According to the archwitch Ndulumi, no one was ever to lay eyes on the msukule; her conditions were violated the moment Wema reentered the shop.

When Mzee Masumbuko and Kisasi realize what happened, they are so disgraced that they flee to a neighboring country. Tunu's grandpa comes to care for Wema and the msukule. For

Tunu's mind is still missing. Though they cut her hair and fingernails, she continues acting like an imbecile. So Grandpa takes Tunu and Wema back to the village of Nyole, to visit the cemetery of their clan. There the locals make a great ritual of slaughtering a donkey and a sheep. They smear Tunu with the blood and make her drink it. Then they drink the blood themselves. Drums are pounded; songs are sung: *Kumpu pu pu pu, kumpu pu pu pu.* Women walk in circles around the fire, chanting, "Tunu is here, Tunu is healed. Thank you mzimu, thank you mzimu." Their ululations praise the clan spirit as they circle the fire. This is the clan's ceremony for bidding farewell to a msukule and welcoming Tunu back to normal, human life.

A hard rain falls. Lightning strikes. The rite goes on. There is a bright, sharp flash next to the grave of Tunu's ancestor, who was once chief. And then the mzimu emerges. His whole body is covered in long strands of hair, except for his eyes, which glow like traffic lights. The mzimu, frightening to behold, speaks in a crackling voice: "Tunu, mjukuu wangu, you are healed and blessed, you and your child and your progeny. But your husband and his wife and their progeny are cursed. Children, take this dawa. Go prepare a night meal and put the dawa in it. Cook and eat it right here, then Tunu will be herself again. There is only one condition: Never return to the house of Tunu's husband, for I have cursed it."

The mzimu vanishes. Two skins sit atop his grave. Wrapped inside are the roots he offered as dawa. They cook a night meal with the dawa and eat it together. Tunu is her whole self again. She and her daughter both swear never to return to the village of Nyangome. They settle down with Grandpa in Nyole and busy themselves farming his plot of land.

One day in the village of Nyole, as Wema and Grandpa are tilling the fields, Wema puts down her hoe and goes to get a drink of water from a clay jug underneath the baobab tree. The tree is in the corner of their plot, where they often rest during breaks. As soon as Wema bends over to draw some water from the jug, she screams, "Mamaaa, I'm dying!"

"Nini tena?" Grandpa's right behind her, ready for a break in the shade. "What's wrong, mjukuu wangu?"

Wema tells him that while she was drawing water, there inside the jug, she had a vision of a msukule with bulging red eyes.

"That's a mirage, Wema dear," Grandpa says. "Water is like a mirror. You see yourself. Just tell me if it ever happens again. I'll find you some dawa and you'll be fine."

Days, months, years pass. They live well and never abandon the habit of eating meals together at night. One evening, as Tunu pounds kisamvu in a mortar, she asks Wema to go buy salt for their night meal. They should sleep soon, since night is falling. Wema reminds her mother, don't they have salt inside? She walks into the dim interior with a kerosene lamp, for there is no electricity in Grandpa's house. An image flashes before her: her mother as a msukule, the way she looked that day in the shop. Then another vision, also a msukule, but different from those she saw in the shop and the water jug: a terrible, incomprehensible face, red eyes blazing like torches, one on each cheek and two more glowing on its forehead. A msukule with cow hooves, green teeth protruding like a boar's, and two horns swarming with twisted, yellow Rasta locks. Its thick pores are perspiring blood. Lost in her visions, Wema watches as the msukule begins to chase her. She stumbles and falls, shouting, crying out, "Mamaaa! Mamamamaaa!"

Tunu startles outside. "What is it, mwanangu?" she rises, calling back to her. "What's going on?"

Grandpa races out of his room, lifting Wema to her feet and consoling her. "Sorry, mjukuu wangu. This darkness is no good. Just wait for the paddy harvest, then I'll get solar panels."

Wema regains her balance. "Thank you, Grandpa. But it's not the dark. It's just, when I came inside, I thought I saw a msukule staring me down, and then it started chasing me."

Grandpa apologizes again. “Don’t worry. I’ll put dawa in your food tonight. We’ll eat together and you won’t have any more of these visions.”

Tunu enters the house to comfort her daughter. She’s carrying their food. They all go back outside and eat a night meal together, with Grandpa’s dawa slipped in.

By the time they finish eating, Wema’s face is strained and wincing. Her eyes bubble up with tears. She clears the dishes, chewing her lips. “Or is it true?” She’s talking to herself, out loud. Her lips quiver like someone overtaken by a chill. “That nothing long is endless, n-no, nothing long is endless.”

Jarupat Petcharawet

Translated from Thai by
Peera Songkünnatham

Jarupat Petcharawet

ความตายของนางเสือง

THE DEATH OF AUNT HUANG

Translated from Thai by
Peera Songkünnatham

The Death of Aunt Huang

Out in the paddy fields, there was a crocodile-bark tree with a knot that never ran dry. Although the liquid oozing from it would solidify into a bead during the dry season, come the first rainfall, that eye-shaped knot, grown out of a score mark carved by Great-Grandpa Sa Buapa, would leak again. It had been leaking like this since forever, so they say. Back when the tree stood strong, kids herding water buffalo would drop by to pick and eat the clear, condensed bead for good fortune and good health in this life and the next.

But today, there's not much good to be found in the paddy plot on which the crocodile-bark tree once stood, much less in the life circumstances of the heir to it, Aunt Huang, who has fallen ill just because she ate a bead from the tree wishing, like those kids, for a good life. Her illness is severe; you could even say she's got one foot in the grave. Two days before the onset of her symptoms, her husband was pestering her to have the tree removed. As he saw it, that tree might come crashing down on somebody once winter rolled in; its brittle, rotting branches could snap and whack them on the noggin; and besides, it was taking direct sunlight away from the rice stalks. At first, she was hesitant, remembering what her father used to say: never cut down this tree. But her husband's insistence prevailed. Plus, E'Paw never let her in on the reason why. He didn't tell her a thing. He loved her so much—too much—that he raised her like a fragile egg that had to be insulated from the world. Aunt Huang married late in life, after her father had already passed, so she loved her husband more than anyone. And so, in the end she gave in and allowed the tree to be chopped down. With the trunk lying on the ground, the bead caught her eye. Reminded of the kids who used to come eat the sap, and the benefits as relayed by their parents, she decided to try it too, in case those benefits could also be hers to enjoy. After the gummy bead had slid down her throat, her older brother Seetone, livid, turned up to harangue her. Gazing at the felled tree, barely able to contain his fury, he bemoaned the coming cataclysm. This wasn't the first time he'd warned her.

"I told her. She didn't listen. And the person she *did* listen to doesn't know jack shit about the history of Bong Woods," Uncle Seetone told his other sister, over puffs of tobacco, after Huang fell ill. He admitted that he was partly to blame; after

E'Paw died, he had been caught up in farmwork and neglected to look after her. He had assumed that she was all grown up, and that E'Paw had already told her some of the backstory of the tree. "The two of them have no idea that the crocodile-bark tree harbors a curse in the eye-shaped knot, that whoever cuts it down is doomed."

"I once told E'Paw that he should hand the paddy plot down to you, Seetone. But he loved his youngest daughter the most. Who knows if Huang has any idea about the power of nature," said Aunt Seenuan as she ground up tongkat ali root and tropical sundew to make a medicinal paste for her sister.

Aunt Huang has been suffering from a strange illness since the beginning of harvest season. Her family brought her to the district hospital multiple times, then the provincial hospital, but no doctor could reach a diagnosis. Her symptoms range from lethargy to occasional delirium—lengthy ravings, sobbing and moaning—like someone possessed by a malevolent spirit. Her brother Seetone went out of his way to hire witch doctor after witch doctor to exorcise the spirit, but no sooner did each of these masters of the occult see her than he would excuse himself, refusing to provide treatment or even counsel. Eight times out of eight, the master left, balls between his legs. Aunt Huang's entire family was terrified. After they gave up on the idea of treatment by magic, many of her relatives could barely bring themselves to visit her at the shack on the paddy, afraid that one of these days the mysterious entity possessing her might just leap to its feet and strangle them. Just a few days later, something of the sort did in fact happen: she squeezed her own neck so hard her face turned green. Seetone and Seenuan lunged at her and tried to unclench her grip, but she wrestled free, knocking them to the ground, then ran to the kitchen end of the shack and grabbed a knife, a rusty old one. Weapon in hand, she proceeded to point it at no one but herself. At her own throat. By the time her brother and sister regained their footing, Aunt Huang had made gashes almost all the way around her neck. Blood flowed from the gaping wounds. Fortunately, the knife was dull, so her arteries weren't nicked. But it was enough to send Huang into shock, her face yellow like a half-ripe mango. Together her two siblings jumped upon her to wrest the knife from her hand. It took them a good while to disarm her. Seetone took the knife outside and flung it across the field; it landed on the other side of the paddy ridge. Seenuan, meanwhile, dragged her sister to the bench-bed; both sisters were bathed crimson. Wrapping herself around her sister like a straitjacket, Seenuan wailed hysterically, while her sister's eyes bulged and stared into space. Seetone stood nearby, catching his breath; he too was blood-stained. His face, furrowed with age, was tense as he watched his two sisters. His brain was muddled. Mere seconds passed before Huang tried to wriggle free from Seenuan's embrace. Even with significant blood loss, Huang still had strength, from god knows where, to overpower her sister, who felt her arm muscles strain and begin to give way. Alarmed, Seetone rushed to Seenuan's aid. He used a loincloth to tie Huang's wrists behind her back, pressed her flat, facedown, on the bed-bench, and used another loincloth to bind her feet together at the ankles. The two were panting by the time they finally tamed her. It took Seetone nearly another half-hour to stanch the flow of blood from Huang's neck.

Several of Huang's relatives paid her a visit later that evening. Small children were prohibited outright from going near her; it didn't matter that she used to be their nice auntie. Meanwhile, her husband, who was not from these parts and who never showed his full face to her relatives, had, just a few days after the onset of her symptoms, already fled from the parched field with a loincloth wrapped around his head like a balaclava.

Before all this, Huang had been a spinster. Her doting father had kept any potential suitor at a distance. Only after the death of her father—the eldest grandchild of Sa Buapa, who had originally cleared this plot of land—did Aunt Huang find love at age forty. None of her relatives knew who the man was or where he was from. He lived with Aunt Huang in her paddy shack for over a year without ever socializing with anyone. Her closest relatives had many theories about him: some said they'd seen him before, here and there in the district center, on the streets, dressed as a mentally ill beggar; others said he looked like one of the police colonels who'd conducted drug raids in the village. But no one had anything conclusive on Aunt Huang's secretive husband, a man alternately perceived as powerful or insane. In any case, he has disappeared from the fields of Bong Woods village. Whether a demon or an angel, the man no longer matters to her relatives or to her. What matters now is finding a way to bring her back.

Three days after Aunt Huang's throat-slitting, Uncle Seetone chanced upon three monks on a pilgrimage along the bank of the Mekong. He had taken his water buffalo to the river's edge for them to have a drink in the overbearing midday heat. The monks' cool, calm demeanors inspired the middle-aged man to kneel on the ground before them, sit with his feet tucked to the side, put his hands together in supplication, and unburden himself to the most senior monk. In the presence of such admirable composure, Uncle Seetone could feel hope well up in him. The senior monk listened to the man's many concerns about his suffering sister while showing neither sympathy nor disregard. He offered a few scriptural teachings and told him to first focus on healing her physical ailments. Leaving aside other issues, which were no less pressing to Huang's kin, the monk stated only that it was the result of karma from her past lives. Uncle Seetone took the monk's words to heart and began to resign himself to what had happened to his little sister. All that remained in his and Seenuan's power was to nurse her messy, self-inflicted knife wounds.

Aunt Seenuan kept an eye on her sister as she mashed up the herbal medicine prescribed by the pilgrim monk, which consisted of tongkat ali root and tropical sundew, a carnivorous plant with blood detoxification properties. She was afraid Huang would stir and reopen the still-tender wounds.

After the incident, Huang's siblings and relatives took her to the district hospital again, this time to be admitted for treatment, but she lasted only one night. With her constant kicking and screaming to let her out of there, her wounds never had a chance to stop their bleeding. The doctor and nurses were at a loss and gave in to her wishes. Besides, seeing as she'd already been on the brink of death well before she slit her throat, the doctor didn't want to keep her away from home.

One night while suffering at home, Aunt Huang raved again for the first time since she'd picked up the rusty knife. As she spoke, tears pooled in the corners of her eyes like the sap leaking from the knot of the crocodile-bark tree. "Brother, Sister, please let me die. Why torture me? The novice wants me dead. *He* held the knife. Slashed my throat with it." Sobs punctuating her voice, she went on, "He wanted me to know what it feels like to have your head cut off."

Shock written on their faces, the two older siblings exchanged uneasy glances. Seenuan, whimpering, turned and stepped outside, leaving Seetone alone in the shack with Huang.

"Who is this novice, Sister?" Seetone asked. Behind his look of worry lurked his hazy knowledge of the *he* Huang was referring to. Grandma and Grandpa on Dad's side had told him about the boy a long time ago.

"It's the ghost of a novice monk inside the crocodile-bark tree. The ghost bound and trapped in there by Great-Grandpa Sa Buapa," Huang struggled to say, careful not to move her lips too much, lest more blood and pus seep from the wounds. Seetone had to keep dabbing them dry with the cotton balls the doctor had provided.

"I see. Speak no more. It'll only worsen the pain. Go to sleep, Sister. Soon you'll get better and be able to play with the kids." As Seetone spoke, he kept his eyes averted from his sister. He was fully aware that his words of consolation were nothing but lies. Years of experience looking after people on their deathbed told him that Huang probably wouldn't survive another three nights. He could only sigh and stay at her side, thinking in the meantime about the novice monk she claimed had slit her throat. He knew that this novice had in fact existed in flesh and blood, that this boy had discovered a secret that Great-Grandpa Sa Buapa had tried to hide, and that the secret had also led Great-Grandpa to inadvertently take Little Novice's life.

Seetone's ancestors weren't originally from Bong Woods. His father had told him that Great-Grandpa Sa Buapa had fled a war on the other side of the Mekong, that he'd dug wells and laid bricks for a new city on this bank. Under the leadership of Mother Khao—the nun who would go on to build Wat Po, the temple housing one of the three emblematic Buddha images of Khemarat Tani—he'd joined people from all walks of life, from monks and nuns and novices to merchants male and female, from villagers and townsfolk to paddy and orchard workers, from singers and storytellers to herb doctors and healers and more, for their exodus. Their city had fallen; their feudal lords had been taken captive; their fellow commoners were being corralled and carted to the lowlands to toil their lives away. Sacred sites had been looted, silver and gold seized. Mother Khao rallied her band of supporters to break through the phalanx of enemy soldiers and into uncharted territory in a bid for survival, a survival synonymous with the refusal to be anyone's slaves or subordinates. As their homeland disintegrated, the tears and blood of their people inundated the river. The metallic scent of death—an utterly humiliating death—permeated the water, its turbid surface turning crimson. Vultures the size of cattle zigzagged in search of corpses felled by the blade. Nighttime echoed with the wails of those who had died unnatural deaths, of spirits turned into starving ghouls looking for offerings of rice from the living. Their cries wormed their way into the ears of those survivors desperately looking for escape routes, depriving them of any respite. As they were preparing a caravan in search of a place to call home, hopefully a fertile land full of grains and greens to harvest, of beasts to hunt and harness, of overflowing abundance that would leave no one hungry, they made rice offerings to the dead to preempt obstacles along the journey ahead. Gathered around Elder Tao Prohm, a dhamma doctor, the people invited their kith and kin who had perished by spear and sword, by hand cannon, matchlock, and flintlock, to come eat and drink to their hearts' content, and entrusted them in turn with protecting the caravan from harm. The elder then officiated a rite for the surviving soldiers and civilians, calling back their spirits from the wilderness and sprinkling their bodies with blessed water to restore their moral and physical health before their departure to the new kingdom of plenty. That night, Elder Tao Prohm inscribed a curse on palm leaves. He damned the invaders to a hellish existence, damned their homeland to a conflagration that would burn for twenty thousand years. Once the elder finished writing—it took over a hundred leaves, each leaf two feet long and two inches wide—the manuscript was bound and flung into the Mekong to keep its contents secret, especially from their wicked foes. Then, the war refugees began the trek downriver. Along the way they ran into several enemy camps, each time facing a great many soldiers. Nonetheless, Mother Khao's caravan successfully fended them off, and eventually put down roots in Kong Paniang, a riverside village later established as the city of Khemarat Tani by the vassal king Jao Kam. There the people lived in peace and happiness for many years.

That is, until Sa Buapa, the youngest grandchild of Elder Tao Prohm and son of Sa Tippahode, the founder of Bong Woods village, spotted the palm-leaf bundle floating down the Mekong. A young fisherman who had inherited the trade from his uncle, Sa Buapa was at first ecstatic—he thought he had come upon a treasure chest belonging to the French, whose army was threatening to take over the land on the other side. But instead, when he untied the bundle, he found two stacks of palm leaves inscribed with words in liturgical Tham script. The first was a cryptic prophecy and call to action. Beckoning the reader to join in its cause, it names a Praya Dhammikaraja, who will bring glory and prosperity to the people. It went on to say that whoever receives the message contained herein must keep it a secret: war will break out on such and such a day of such and such a month; you must keep your doors shut; do not light any torches lest you lead someone your way; do not respond to greetings or calls for help. Warning: Non-believers will see great destruction befall their lives and their possessions; believers will prosper and live to a thousand years old. The other text, radically different in tone and message, was full of hate and vindictiveness, of curse words the likes of which Sa Buapa had never heard before. Each unholy term was directed at a group of people who were left unnamed, but he had some idea who they might be. Summed up, the curse went: May the destroyers of our homeland be met with ruin. It read like a sorcerer's incantation, a sutra of black magic—a subject he knew a bit about, as he had studied it on the sly. Based on his knowledge, he was sure the text was an abomination that should be kept from human eyes. Back when he'd studied Pali at the temple, he'd only encountered religious texts—no palm leaf ever contained words like these. If he wasn't reading about the Buddha's life or about His penultimate lifetime as Pra Vessantara, he was studying herbal medicinal formulas or Brahman sutras for officiating communal rites. So, to prevent the unholy text from falling into anyone else's hands, Sa Buapa decided to burn it. He built a fire and threw in the palm leaves. As the fire blazed Sa Buapa heard a wail, a collective wail of thousands of people resounding over the great, wide river.

He looked around, panicking. In that moment, the sky darkened over the water; wind and rain suddenly bore down on the spot. Sa Buapa had to scramble away to take cover. The following morning, he returned to the site of the fire. Halfway down the riverbank, he spotted a novice monk unfolding and poring over one of the partially burnt manuscripts. Sa Buapa went white as a sheet, fearful the little novice would share its contents with others. The fisherman darted across the bank to snatch the text from Little Novice's hands, all the while screaming, "Don't read it!" But Little Novice ignored his warning, glared at him, and took off running with the whole bundle. Sa Buapa pursued him, trying his hardest to catch up. But as he ran, he felt something grab ahold of his legs. He had to stop and mouth a mantra to banish the mysterious force holding him back. He resumed chasing the stubborn monk-in-training, finally catching up with him on the tip of land where a river mouth fed into the Mekong, an area full of fallen logs, roots and all, that had been washed ashore. Having cornered Little Novice, Sa Buapa pounced on him. Nimbly, the novice ducked, then dodged sideways, looking all the while for an opening to scuttle away.

"Now, now, give it to me. Novice, you are a child. You're too young to read this stuff," said Sa Buapa as he launched forward, catching air instead of the boy. "It's no good at all. It's for ghouls, for people eaters... Give it to me!"

"No! I'm taking it to Grandpa Reverend. Have him take a look and tell me what it is."

"Absolutely not! Grandpa Reverend mustn't see it," he said, alarmed by the novice's mention of the old monk as his mind put two and two together: in a meeting at the temple the other day, he'd heard the reverend and everyone else, from ordinary villagers to the local ruler, say the name Praya Dhammikaraja—the name he'd read in the manuscripts, who would bring glory and prosperity to the land. These people are about to foment a rebellion, he realized.

"Please, Novice. It's an abomination. It shouldn't exist. Not in this land," he said, and then lunged at Little Novice, who was standing on a ledge jutting out over the confluence. This time, he successfully grabbed the bundle of palm leaves, but his body also crashed into the novice's torso, knocking him off the edge and straight into the river mouth below. His saffron robe fluttering, Little Novice was impaled midair by a fallen log whose roots as big as arms stuck out like quills on a porcupine. He died instantly. Bright red blood spurted onto the saffron robe. One of the roots, sharp as a rhino horn, had entered under his chin and exited through his nape. From his mouth, gobs of blood spilled into the confluence, streaking the Mekong crimson. Sa Buapa was dumbstruck with horror. His face turned ghastly pale, as if he were at death's door. He stood there trembling. The stacks of palm leaves fell to the ground with a thud, although he barely noticed the cryptic curse slipping out of his hands.

For a good while, the fisherman hesitated over what to do with Little Novice's dead body. He looked over his shoulder, anxious of being seen by the folks who came to the river in the morning to fish, forage for food and firewood, or pick the cabbages and the capers they'd planted along the bank. But it was cold that morning, and there was no one to be seen. His mind made up, Sa Buapa carried the novice's robed body to his rowboat at the dock, snapped off tree branches, covered the entire body with them, and began rowing northward upstream. He was headed toward a dense forest not frequented by foragers, as it was home to an ambush of tigers. (Tiger Cave Jungle would later become the rice fields that Sa Buapa passed on to his eldest son, Aunt Huang's paternal grandfather, who passed it on to her father, who then passed it on to her.) With few daring to enter, the jungle was well suited for hiding a crime such as this.

Sa Buapa buried the novice's body together with the palm-leaf manuscripts near a rosewood tree. Afterward, he rowed downstream back to the dock at Kong Paniang. As the boat neared the shore, he caught sight of monks, novices, laypeople—nearly the entire village. They made a terrible racket calling out the name Little Novice Panna. Some of them were poking around tall clumps of grass and bushes; others searched along the riverbank; others still were dipping in and out of the water around the river mouth. The fisherman's blood ran cold. His hands shook, and he stared blankly, as if in a trance. A long moment passed before he finally drove the boat forward and, using a hemp rope, tied the boat to a stump on the shore. As soon as he finished mooring, several of the villagers hurtled toward him and asked, in rapid succession, about Little Novice Panna, their voices quivering. One of them was the novice's father. At first, Sa Buapa was flustered, but he answered each of their questions calmly, without arousing any suspicion. He told them how he'd been out since daybreak to retrieve the gillnets he had set in the stretch of the river by Tiger Cave Jungle. No, he hadn't seen anyone on the riverbank. No, he didn't know that Little Novice usually came here—quite a ways from the temple—to fetch water with a bucket. Why would he come all the way here? As Sa Buapa laid out his answers, the father and the others were left crestfallen. They could only ask the fisherman to join the search. The villagers were talking within earshot: "Maybe Little Novice fell into the Mekong and drowned, as the only trace of him is his resin-caulked bamboo bucket sitting next to the cabbage beds along the dock. Could be that a siren lured him into the river, that's happened before." Hearing this theory, the fisherman breathed a sigh of relief.

He also felt a touch of pride for having had the prudence to remove the log that had impaled the novice, by prying and pushing it out into a whirlpool in the river mouth. The blood had faded and become one with the turbid water, leaving no trace for the villagers to find. Well, who can help him when he was basically asking to get himself killed, Sa Buapa thought to himself.

Once the father and the rest of the group left, the fisherman pretended for a while to help look for Little Novice. But he kept coming up empty, of course, whether clearing his way through the tall grass along the bank or diving through the muddy water, so he slowly broke away. He returned home and performed a rite to ask for forgiveness from the spirit of Little Novice Panna, praying for the dead to absolve him of the karma he had set in motion, because the whole thing had been an accident; he hadn't intended to take the novice's life. Plus, it was Little Novice who had meddled in this affair no one was supposed to know about. It was an abomination. And if His Majesty the King and his ministers were to hear about it, they would certainly not be happy.

Sa Buapa set out the instruments of black magic with which to bind Novice Panna's spirit, to keep it from coming after him and his family. He planned on leaving the body in the ground for three years; only after that would he exhume it for a proper cremation with rice offerings to set Little Novice on a path toward a good birth and happiness in the next lifetime. The fisherman spent the early evening finding the needed instruments. At the auspicious hour, he retreated to the back room reserved for performing rites and began mouthing a mantra he had studied in monkhood. During the chant, however, a gust of wind burst into the room, knocking over the ritual copper bowl and the pedestal tray of flowers and scattering their contents everywhere. The candle and incense were extinguished and had to be relit. But Sa Buapa did not give up. Fighting the relentless wind, he took pains to restart the rite over and over again. And every so often the chilly blasts carried a whiff of blood, a metallic dampness that rushed into his lungs. On top of that, a strange chorus of wails assailed him from every direction, giving him goosebumps all over. Sa Buapa fretted the whole time he was chanting and couldn't concentrate. There was no sign that the situation would be resolved. He paused the rite to say a benediction, to no avail: "May all beings be free from enmity, from malice, from physical or mental suffering; may they be happy and free from harm." Equally useless was his attempt to recite a chant against saboteurs. Despite the cold draft, Sa Buapa was drenched in sweat. He felt as if he were running up Krajiew Mountain. Eventually, he gave up. Lying in bed, hand on forehead, he puzzled over how to handle Little Novice's spirit before it grew even angrier.

He fell asleep. In his dream, he saw Little Novice Panna out and about, airing the contents of the palm-leaf manuscripts to anyone who would listen. The novice spoke in measured syllables as if reciting a magic spell, and all those listening to him were the living, from the local ruler and Grandpa Reverend to Novice Panna's father and the other villagers who'd gone looking for him that day. Then, the dream cut to a throng of people coming from all directions to point fingers and hurl curses at him, Sa Buapa. They called on the plague to chew his liver and lungs to pieces. Called him a sick, heinous, nation-forsaking bastard for attempting to bury the truth, a scoundrel ignorant of his own roots and ungrateful to the progenitors of mankind Grandpa Sankasa and Grandma Sankasee. Damned him to be boiled alive in the Cauldron of Hell. Sa Buapa woke up screaming at the crack of dawn, startling his wife who lay next to him. The fisherman, soaked in cold sweat from head to toe, deflected his wife's questions and hurried down the ladder of the house, saying he was going to retrieve his gillnets, when in reality he hadn't gone near his fishing spot since the previous morning. Sa Buapa quickened his steps, having decided to dig up the novice's body and burn it. A spirit this mighty and malevolent cannot be allowed to roam, he thought. He was convinced that it was the curse on those palm leaves that had made Little Novice's spirit so vicious—and even before the night was through. The previous evening, he had performed a simple rite, designed to lock up an ordinary spirit, thinking it would do to prevent the novice from visiting people in their dreams and divulging the secret. It had failed. The ghost of Little Novice had grown too powerful. He had underestimated the severity of the situation. A spirit so vicious could only be defeated by the most potent of anti-demonic spells.

Sa Buapa furiously dug up the grave. He swung his hoe, not caring where it landed or what body part it might cut up. Once the corpse, now stiff and bloated, was uncovered, he wrenched a Lost Dog vine from a tree, tied it around Novice Panna's neck, and hauled the body out of the pit in a fit of rage. He handled the body roughly, as if it were a pig's or a dog's carcass, as if the deceased were a wild beast with no family or friends. The powers of a Lost Dog vine can reach both the living and the dead. The living who inadvertently walk over it while hiking through the forest will lose their sense of direction and walk in circles until they succumb to injuries or illness, or they might cross the threshold into a hidden, ghost-guarded realm, never to return to the human world. As for the dead noosed with the vine, they will be hopelessly trapped inside the dark walls of magic erected by their mortal enemy.

Not that Sa Buapa was all that bent on revenge: he bore no real grudge against the novice, but he had to follow every step of the Brahman ritual to ensure its effectiveness. It was a sacred ritual; carelessly performed, it would only backfire.

Sa Buapa then built a large pyre. Orange flames spun and leapt above a clearing of flat rock in the jungle. A plume of smoke rose into the sky. Wild birds, startled, took flight and disappeared far away from the pyre. Soon, the body once robed in saffron was charred black. Firewood from a newly dead gurjan tree burns at a high temperature; it is used primarily in blacksmithing, to make knives, machetes, axes, spades, and the like, so when one uses it to cremate a body, it burns it up in a matter of seconds. The fire left only the boy's ashes. Sa Buapa proceeded to extinguish the embers with water from a natural basin in the rock, sweep the white bits of skull and skeleton into the basin, pestle everything into a fine powder, spoon the bone dust into a cup molded out of lac, recite the required incantation three times, and then head to a crocodile-bark tree deeper in the jungle. The tree has a local name, chüak, meaning rope; it belongs to the same class of plants, symbolically speaking, as sword grass, whose blades are used to transfix roaming spirits that attack people. But the rope tree is reserved for use against spirits of the recently deceased. Sa Buapa gouged out a hole in the trunk, shoved the cup containing the novice's ashes inside, and repeated the incantation again while walking in circles around the trunk until, more than 300 laps later, he was certain the spirit had lost all sense of direction within the walls of magic. Only then did he leave Tiger Cave Jungle.

Seetone pauses his recollection here to heave a mournful sigh as he looks at his little sister. The brunt of that karma has fallen on her, the heir to the paddy plot that used to be Tiger Cave Jungle. Great-Grandpa Sa Buapa died soon after emerging from the jungle that day; a group of revolutionaries who called themselves the Meritful Persons ganged up on him by the Mekong and summarily stomped him to death for betraying his clan. In the years since, Tiger Cave Jungle was progressively cleared and cut into paddy plots by Seetone's grandfather's generation, until it was razed flat during his dad's youth, when chainsaws and sawmills were introduced to the city of Khemarat, now a mere provincial district. Of the smattering of trees that remain, only a few species provide shade during the planting and harvest seasons. The crocodile-bark tree was one such species, until this harvest season, when the last one standing behind Aunt Huang's shack was felled—a decision that Seetone believes ultimately caused his youngest sister's illness.

Seetone recalls his grandpa telling him about the crocodile-bark tree in the time after Great-Grandpa's passing: from the knife mark, two bulges appeared, like a pair of human eyes.

What's strange was that one of them, the one looking East, began leaking a tear-like liquid all year long, while the one looking West closed up and fused into the gray scaly bark. Come dry season, the discharge from the open eye would solidify into beads of colorless resin as lustrous as a raindrop. One day, a boy herded his water buffalo to graze along the perimeter of this woodland. With the sweltering heat emanating from the sunbaked earth, he suddenly became thirsty. Without a machete to score a sabaeng branch for drinking water, he looked around and caught sight of the shiny bead on the eye of the crocodile-bark tree, and proceeded to pluck it and chew it to quench his thirst. In the days afterward, the boy kept returning to the tree, piquing the curiosity of the other buffalo-herd boys. They asked, and he told them. From then on, every one of them would regularly sneak off to the tree to pick a resin bead to eat. The boys said with one voice that eating it boosted their energy, reading skills, and appetite, such that a regular dish of rice and fish now tasted as sweet and as smooth as overripe bananas. What's more, they slept well and dreamed of the Kingdom of Pra Sri Ariya Maitreya, and of the spheres of Heaven all the way up to the sixteen Brahma realms. Hearing this, the grownups were amused and chuckled among themselves. These kids, they figured, probably just took the sermon they heard every Buddhist Lent a bit too seriously. So they didn't pay them much attention. Nor did they suspect anything when, one Buddhist Lent, the boys who had eaten from the crocodile-bark tree all decided to take a vow to become novices. In fact, their parents wholeheartedly gave their blessings; they even set up an altar for the community to make offerings to the newly ordained. The paddy plot continued to yield abundant crops; never were there any incidents of a forest god or paddy ghost making an appearance to harm the owner of this patch of land, generation after generation. Only when Aunt Huang had the crocodile-bark tree cut down was misfortune let loose, and her fatal illness is the result.

At sundown, amid the whirring flutters of giant leaf bugs signaling a drought that will last for weeks upon weeks, Seetone makes a fire. In addition to steaming rice and grilling fish, he's going to boil some rice water on the off chance his little sister will swallow a few drops. As he busies himself in front of the clay brazier, his gaze can't help wandering over to the dirt track through the fields, made by walk-behind tractors—he's heard from his sister Seenuan that several of their nieces and nephews are coming to keep vigil at Huang's bedside. He keeps glancing that direction, until, over the brazier, the bamboo cone emits jets of steam, exuding the aroma of sticky rice ready to be flipped upside down for an even cook, but even then, nobody shows, nobody except for Seenuan, his sister, twin sister in fact, the person who push-kicked him into the world. She has returned from the village with an armful of food in plastic bags purchased from a motorcycle grocer, all Seetone's favorites, from spiced fermented meat and salted fish eggs to the divine vegetable sauce made by Miss Samlee, an ex-girlfriend of his who has a stall in the district's central market. The sight of all this food makes his stomach growl, but the man isn't sure if in his current mood he'll be able to swallow.

Barely has he finished fluffing up the rice and putting it in a container than Aunt Huang suddenly goes into spasms. She thrashes around, her eyes bulging as if about to pop out. Her feet sweep medicines and utensils off the bench-bed, and they fall with a kerplunk on the floor. And her raving picks up where it left off last time. The two older siblings have to jump in and pin her down.

"He's here! The novice is here! Help me, Brother, Sister. I can't anymore. He's pulling my head so hard he's about to rip it off!" Huang launches into a tirade against the novice, but soon switches her tone, crying out, "Don't hurt him, poor boy, he has nobody left..." Then she squeezes her neck, causing fresh blood to ooze from the scabs. Her convulsing body tenses from head to toe. In tears, Seenuan restrains her sister as Seetone quickly ties her up with a loincloth. It takes every last bit of their combined strength to pacify her. Wordlessly, Seetone and Seenuan look at their sister who, frozen in terror, does not return their gaze. The brother shakes his head slowly. He feels a sickness creeping up on him, inching him closer and closer to her helpless condition. As he contemplates her withered frame, he drifts in and out of a trance. Images Huang described the other day flash through his mind. He tries to will them away, but they intrude into his inner eye again and again, with each and every breath.

The night after Aunt Huang ate the bead from the crocodile-bark tree, she dreamed she came across a novice monk behind her shack, untying a vine from around his own neck. With piety, she knelt and bowed to the ground before the novice, who seized the opportunity to tie that same vine around her neck. "Walk us to the dock!" he barked. Bewildered, Huang froze and, through inaction, resisted his command. Little Novice then yanked the vine, nearly suffocating her. Her two hands, still free, tried in vain to loosen the vine. Little Novice pulled at it again; this time she felt as if her head was being torn clean off. The vine dug into her flesh, stabbing her neck all the way around. She coughed, rose to her feet, and started walking as told. She didn't dare turn to ask him where exactly they were headed. Little Novice himself said little other than to command her to walk faster. Several times, he shoved her so hard she fell on her face, and then he'd snarl, "Get up! Quick!" But she couldn't go any faster with the vine choking her, so Little Novice took the lead and dragged her by the neck, raking her limbs through the thorny brambles under the scorching dry-season sun. Once they reached the dock, the novice pushed her onto a boat and threw her a paddle: "Upstream. My people are waiting. Quickly or we won't make it in time to help them." The novice tugged on the vine like he was a cattleman pulling a water buffalo by its nose into the slaughterhouse. Wheezing and panting, Huang struggled to paddle. But somehow, her slowness didn't affect the boat's speed. On the contrary, the more slowly she paddled, the more swiftly the boat charged forward against the current. Suddenly she smelled something nauseating coming from the water, an odor so putrid that she dry heaved. She looked down at the river, trying to find its source, and was about to turn to ask the novice when she heard sobbing coming from the bow where he sat. Her tormentor was crying. Wiping his tears, he said, "They've killed all of our people—every single one. There's nothing left, not a roof, not a floorboard." In that instant, Huang's heart shook. She didn't know what was going on. Why was he crying? Who had been killed? "Our" people? She was confounded. And why was the novice acting differently now? The mean, angry person who'd dragged her down here by the neck was now a bawling child at the boat's bow. He bawled like there was no tomorrow, his lips and neck quivering, his face drained of color. He shook his head side to side like a man with nothing to his name. A moment later, Huang felt around her neck and was surprised to find no vine there. Freed from her collar, she decided to head toward the shore while offering the novice occasional words of sympathy. As she trailed the paddle on one side to steer the boat toward the shore, the wide river suddenly turned crimson, the air heavy with a gamey smell. She flinched, sending the boat rocking stern to bow. The entire river was the color of blood; headless corpses bobbed on the surface. In the sky, vultures and crows circled and zigzagged. Witnessing the scene, the novice sobbed even harder. He recited a benediction through his tears. Huang was speechless, horrified by the image before her. Who, who committed this savagery? Looking toward the shore, she was horrified to see a great number of soldiers restraining and beheading villagers. The heads they pitched onto boats; the bodies they threw into the water. In utter shock, Huang felt her instinct to flee kick in; she planted the paddle deep in the water to lever the boat away, but then she glimpsed a familiar face waving to her from among the soldiers. She stared at him and tried to think. She could faintly hear him shout: "Huang, come back. It's me. Don't be afraid. Just paddle to the shore. I'm with them, they're not going to harm you. Don't you recognize me? It's Sarge Kan, your husband." Huang squinted for a better look. It was indeed her husband, Sergeant Kan. But she hesitated. Turning to the novice, she asked him whether they should approach. He gave no response except for a look of despair, which unsettled her deeply. She knew—believed—that she'd be safe among those people, but what about *him*? Were they going to hurt the novice? Then it occurred to her: the novice was a disciple of the Lord Buddha; after all, her husband was human, and a devout Buddhist too, so the soldiers with him shouldn't be so heartless as to kill the novice in cold blood. She decided then to paddle to the shore where her husband stood. As the boat made its way there, she could hear more and more clearly the yells of soldiers terrorizing her neighbors. Then the boat beached. As soon as the novice stood up at the bow, a spear shot out from the throng of soldiers, pierced through his chin, and exited through his nape. His body collapsed in a heap of saffron. Blood spurted as if from a burst dam, rushing over the boat's sides and spilling into the Mekong. Shuddering, Huang let out a shrill scream as the soldiers crowed with satisfaction.

Huang fainted, and when she came to, most of the soldiers had already dispersed from that length of the shore. She counted no more than ten men, all burly. They were forcing twenty, thirty women onto the boats, each with a pile of human heads on board, and were ordering their captives to go hawk the trophies to people on the other side of the river. These women were all from Huang's village. The sight turned her stomach. She sprinted to her husband, who was piling up the boats with her people's humiliation, and told him to stop harassing her friends and neighbors. He refused. He had to follow his superior's orders; disobedience only meant his head would be next to roll. At her wits' end, she approached the highest-ranking officer at the scene, who was giving out orders, and prostrated herself at his feet. Her pleas only irritated him, and he ordered her husband and some other soldiers to take her away, and if she disobeyed and kept running her mouth, to cut out her tongue.

Eventually, the women were forced at gunpoint to paddle the boats loaded with the heads of their relatives from this side of the river and sell them to their relatives on the other side. On each boat were two women, one the paddler, the other the crier whose task it was to tout their wares—a tactic designed to strike fear into the hearts of people on the other bank, to make it easier to tyrannize them later. The women on each boat carried out their jobs in tears. The soldiers, including Huang's husband, kept watch farther behind. Whenever someone disobeyed, she, along with her partner, would be executed by flintlock and pushed overboard. Witnessing this from the opposite shore, Huang sobbed and gasped and thrashed in the sand as though she were dying of suffocation.

Tears fall from Seetone's face as he watches a convulsing Huang take her last gasp of air. In sorrow, he gazes at his youngest sister, now departed, never to return. Seenuan is inconsolable. Outside, in the darkness, cold air envelops the paddy shack. An icy gust enters the shack, carrying with it a mysterious wail that echoes deep inside Seetone, the person long privy to the truth. That wail resounds through the waters and the skies. It's still resounding through those waters and skies...

Contributors

Wajdi al-Ahdal, born in 1973, is a Yemeni novelist and author of short stories and plays. His twenty published works have been translated into English, French, Italian, Spanish, Russian, and Turkish. His novels available in English translation are *A Land Without Jasmine* (Garnet, 2012) and *Land of Sweetheart Deals* (DarArab, 2024). His short story "The Slow Man" appeared in *Banthology: Stories from Banned Nations* (Deep Vellum Publishing, 2018).

Brian Bergstrom is a Montréal-based lecturer and translator. His translations have appeared in publications including *Granta*, *Aperture*, *LitHub*, *Mechademia*, *The Penguin Book of Japanese Short Stories*, and *Elemental: Earth Stories*. His translation of *Trinity, Trinity, Trinity* by Erika Kobayashi (Astra House, 2022) won the 2022 Japan–U.S. Friendship Commission (JUSFC) Prize for the Translation of Japanese Literature. His most recent translation is *Slow Down: The Degrowth Manifesto* (Astra House, 2024) by Marxist philosopher Kōhei Saitō.

Cho Yeeun, born in 1993, is a South Korean writer. She won the Excellence Prize at the 2016 Goldenbough Time Leap Fiction Contest with the short story “오버랩 나이프, 나이프” [Overlapped knife, knife] and the Grand Prize at the 4th Kyobo Story Contest with the novel 시프트 [Shift] (2017). She is the author of *The New Seoul Park Jelly Massacre* (tr. English by Yewon Jung, Honford Star 2024), 스노볼 드라이브 [Snowglobe drive] (2021), 트로피컬 나이트 [Tropical night] (2022), 테디베어는 죽지 않아 [Teddy bear never dies] (2023), and 적산가옥의 유령 [The haunting of the enemy’s house] (2024).

Thórdís Helgadóttir is an Icelandic writer whose work has earned critical acclaim and accolades in Iceland and abroad, including nominations for the Nordic Council Literature Prize and the Icelandic Literature Prize. She writes poetry, fiction, and drama. Thórdís is a member of the Svikaskáld writers’ collective and coeditor of the literary magazine *Stelkur*, as well as a creative writing teacher. She doesn’t believe in ghosts, yet they haunt her work aggressively.

Tomoyuki Hoshino is a novelist and essayist who has won most of the major literary prizes in Japan, including the Bungei Prize, the Mishima Yukio Prize, the Noma Literary New Face Prize, and the Ōe Kenzaburō Prize. *Honō (焔)* [The fire], the collection from which this story is taken, won the Tanizaki Prize in 2018.

William Hutchins was born on the campus of Berea College and studied there. He holds degrees from Yale University and the University of Chicago. He has taught at the Gerard School in Lebanon, the University of Ghana, the American University in Cairo, and the University of Angers in France. A former National Endowment for the Arts Fellow, Hutchins is a Professor Emeritus at Appalachian State University.

Lusajo Mwaikenda Israel is a Tanzanian writer who received his degree in fine and performing arts from the University of Dar es Salaam. He further pursued his master's in Community Economic Development at Open University of Tanzania and a post-graduate diploma in Education at Teofilo Kisanji University. His writing appears in *No Edges: Swahili Stories.* He was a founding member of Daz Nundaz, a pioneering group of the Bongo Flava/Swahili hip-hop musical genres.

Sabrina Jaszi is a literary translator based in Alameda, CA, working from Uzbek, Ukrainian, and Russian. Her published translations include the works of Salomat Vafo, Suhbat Aflatuni, O'tkir Hoshimov, Reed Grachev, Nadezhda Teffi, and Alisa

Ganieva. Her co-translation with Roman Ivashkiv of Andriy Sodomora's *The Tears and Smiles of Things* (Academic Studies Press) received the American Association for Ukrainian Studies' Best Translation Prize for 2023–24. She is also a writer with stories and essays published in *StoryQuarterly*, *J Journal*, *The Paris Review Daily*, and elsewhere. She is the co-founder of Turkoslavia, a collective and journal devoted to Turkic and Slavic literature in translation. To learn more, visit Turkoslavia.com.

Anna Kańtoch is a prolific, much-awarded, multi-genre Polish author with many successful full-length standalone novels, book series, and short-story anthologies to her name. An alumna of the Jagiellonian University and based in Katowice in Silesia, Kańtoch is a member of the Harda Horda [Hardy Horde] all-female speculative fiction literary group. "Krok przed tobą" appeared in the group's *Harde Baśnie* [Hardy Tales] anthology (SQN, 2020).

Larissa Kyzer is a writer and Icelandic–English literary translator. Her translation work has been supported by the National Endowment for the Arts, the European Union Prize for Literature, Fulbright, the American–Scandinavian Foundation, the Icelandic Literature Center, Reykjavík UNESCO City of Literature, and Finland's Kone Foundation. She is a member of the Translators Organizing Committee, on the board of the American Literary Translators Association, and runs the Women+ in Translation reading series Jill!

Kasia Laganowska is bilingual, bicultural, and binational. An alumna of Cambridge University and based in the UK, she translates between Polish and English. Kasia most enjoys working with verse and quirky mainstream prose, especially speculative fiction. She was selected for the Emerging Translator Mentorship run by the UK National Centre for Writing and is a member of the Society of Authors.

Jarupat Petcharawet is a writer from northeastern Thailand who lives in the fields outside his home village close to the Mekong. His fiction is notable for its realistic worldbuilding and its bold use of the vernacular language—and along with that, vernacular understandings of nonhuman powers. Jarupat is most known for อีกา [Crow] (2017), his debut collection of stories of rural doom, which offers a fresh spin on ancient Lao apocalyptic literature.

Richard Prins is a New Yorker who has lived, worked, studied, and recorded music in Dar es Salaam. Forthcoming books include *Brain Flavor: A Lyric History of Swahili Hip Hop* (No University

Press), *We May Eat Fruit* (Ghostbird Press), and his translation of the Swahili novel *Walenisi* (University of Georgia Press), which received a 2023 PEN/Heim Translation Fund Grant and 2024 NEA Translation Fellowship. His work also appears in *The Best American Essays 2024*.

Giulia Ratti is a translator from Italy. After an MA at SOAS and a stint as an anxious office worker, she attended LTI Korea and translated Cho Yeeun's *Cocktail, Love, Zombie* during her ALTA mentorship with Janet Hong. Her translation of Cho Yeeun's "Invitation" was published in *The Offing*. She loves horror books and taking walks with her just-as-anxious dog. She also translates authors such as Sang Young Park and Won-pyung Sohn into Italian.

Peera Songkünnatham is a translator from Sisaket City, northeastern Thailand. Currently based in Indianapolis, Peera works between English, Thai, Spanish, and Isan, a mix of Lao and Thai from their home region. They run the website Sanam Ratsadon: An Archive of Common(er) Feelings, which showcases Thai literary artifacts of political significance that would otherwise not circulate in translation.

Salomat Vafo is a writer and journalist from the Xorazm region of western Uzbekistan. An irrepressible force in Uzbek literature since the 1980s, Vafo has been called fearless and merciless. She writes about ordinary people at the edges of her country, as well as those who have slipped over the edges—because of shifting borders, punishing gender norms, environmental destruction, or the necessity of foreign migrant work. In 2004, with *Tilsim saltanati* [The Empire of Secrets], she became the first woman to publish a novel in Uzbek. A 2009 fellow of the University of Iowa's International Writers' Program, Vafo has been translated into German, Turkish, and Russian. She lives in Tashkent. Two English translations of her short stories have appeared in *The Dial.*

'Twas
Alive Here
Once

Ghost Stories

Other titles in the Calico Series

That We May Live: Speculative Chinese Fiction

Home: Arabic Poems

Elemental: Earth Stories

Cuíer: Queer Brazil

This Is Us Losing Count: Eight Russian Poets

Visible: Text + Image

No Edges: Swahili Stories

Elektrik: Caribbean Writing

Through the Night Like a Snake: Latin American Horror Stories

Cigarettes Until Tomorrow: Romanian Poetry

Unusual Fragments: Japanese Stories

Hair on Fire: Afghan Women Poets

CALICO

The Calico Series, published biannually by Two Lines Press, captures vanguard works of translated literature in stylish, collectible editions. Each Calico is a vibrant snapshot that explores one aspect of our present moment, offering the voices of previously inaccessible, highly innovative writers from around the world today.